I0757987

Twins

Anders Björklund

Copyright © 2025 Anders Björklund

All Rights Reserved

eBook ISBN: 978-1-966931-61-4

Paperback ISBN: 978-1-966931-62-1

Hardback ISBN: 978-1-966931-63-8

Preface

What we perceive as dark matter is all the matter that exists in parallel universes to our own universe. All the matter in our universe is perceived as dark matter in the other parallel universes. Matter in the different universes cannot interact with particles from others. We in our universe cannot see or sense the matter in other universes, and the same applies to the other universes, but the parallel worlds exist in the same space as ours.

There are a total of six universes. Ours makes up 5% of the matter, and the other parallel universes 27%, and in a living being, the soul consists of matter. When a being dies, the mass of the soul converts into energy (hence the weight loss) and can travel freely to a random universe. There, the energy converts back into mass, forming a soul in a new life.

$E = mc^2$

Anders Björklund

Somewhere Else

Lying on his back, Mikael opened his small blue eyes and was met by a dark purple sky framed by thick, tall, swaying blades of grass. He listened to the soothing sound of the wind as it made the meadow dance in a gentle, undulating rhythm, and he realized he was no longer in the Timmerlunda Forest.

He remembered the scarf he had been trying to free from the rock wall just moments ago and how it had sparked and coiled around his hand, refusing to let him go. After that, he woke up somewhere else.

Slowly, he sat up and noticed the scarf in his hand. Now, it was back to being just an ordinary scarf again, and as he opened his hand, it slipped slowly to the ground and settled neatly in place.

He grabbed a handful of the tall grass blades and pulled them toward himself. He couldn't recall seeing grass like this before.

The stalk was much thicker than ordinary grass yet supple, and the top was crowned with a single large dangling seed head. The ground he had been lying on was made of shimmering green soil, unlike anything he had ever seen. Yes, he was certain now—this was not the Timmerlunda Forest.

He stood up and saw the rock wall behind him. It resembled the one where the scarf had been stuck, yet it was different. Here, the rock had a completely different color and texture. It was much darker—almost black—and significantly rougher, like the charcoal his father used during their barbecue evenings back home.

He looked up at the sky again to take in the dark purple expanse. The stars shone brightly above, and it was night, just like at home. But as he stood there all alone, gazing at the unfamiliar night sky, fear began to creep into him. Only now did he fully grasp that something very strange had happened and that he might never see his brother again. From now on, he would have to manage completely on his own—a twelve-year-old boy without his very best friend.

His twin brother, Peter.

The First Journey

Chapter 1

Peter first turned the envelope over to see if there was a sender. After confirming the back was blank, he slid his index finger into the small opening on one edge of the envelope and carefully tore it open. He pulled out the contents and began reading the letter.

I'M ALIVE, BUT I CAN'T GET BACK.

IF YOU'RE READING THIS, PLEASE RESCUE ME.

GO TO THE CAMPING SPOT AND WAIT FOR AN OPENING IN THE ROCK; YOU'LL KNOW IT WHEN YOU SEE IT.

MICKE

It's the middle of June 1987, and Peter is sitting on his couch in his apartment, reading the letter. Not a day has gone by without him thinking about Mikael, his twin brother, who disappeared that night ten years ago while they were camping with Filip. Those were the last days of the best summer vacation ever.

The summer vacation with his beloved twin brother Mikael and their best friend, Filip. The summer vacation with a capital "S." They were twelve years old, and after the break, everything was going to change—they'd be moving up to middle school, where they'd suddenly become the youngest again.

It had been the best summer vacation ever until that Saturday morning in mid-August when Peter and Filip woke up in the tent to discover Mikael's sleeping bag was empty.

Peter and Mikael were always together, inseparable. They slept together, ate together, fought together. Like two little puppies constantly bickering, only to fall asleep in a heap on the floor. It was always the two of them, every minute of every day, and since they were identical twins, they looked exactly alike. But that's where the similarities ended.

Peter was more thoughtful and sensible, while Mikael was impulsive, often not considering the consequences of his actions. This also made him the more inventive one.

At school, Mikael proved to be exceptionally talented in art. Some of his drawings were displayed throughout the school, which made him extremely proud. Peter, on the other hand, excelled in core subjects like Swedish, English, and math—areas Mikael struggled with, especially spelling, which was downright dreadful.

With the letter still in his hand, Peter sat frozen on the couch, completely still, as if time itself had stopped. He read the letter repeatedly, but the words seemed to float aimlessly on the paper. He couldn't grasp the context or the message. The shock of what he'd apparently read and understood the first time now rendered the text incomprehensible. For a moment, he wondered if it might be a joke.

Who had sent the letter?

The letter had arrived in a standard postal envelope. The address to Peter was written on a yellow adhesive label, the kind used for mail forwarding. Turning over the letter, he saw the address of their home from ten years ago: Småkulle Street 2, Timmerlunda.

A year after Mikael's disappearance, the family had moved from Timmerlunda to the larger town of Rågmanstorp.

When Peter turned nineteen, he moved out to a small one-bedroom apartment where he now lived. He hadn't finished high school, dropping out to work at the paper mill in Bofsnäs instead. Ever since Mikael's disappearance, Peter had struggled with concentration. He felt a constant sense of something—or someone—missing in his life. Focusing on work at the mill was easier than sitting in a classroom.

Who would send a letter in Mikael's name asking for help if not Mikael himself? No one!

Peter placed the letter on the coffee table, taking care to avoid the remnants of the previous day's pizza and a dozen empty beer cans. He stood up and walked to the window, hoping to clear his mind. Outside, in the distance, he saw the forest, mountains, and vast open spaces. The sight reminded him of the forest and mountains where they had spent most of Mikael's last summer.

He and Mikael...

...and Filip.

Peter, Micke, and Fille.

The three twelve-year-old boys—Peter, Mikael, and Filip—walked side by side along the gravel road leading out of Timmerlunda, as they had done so many times that summer. But this time would be their very last. It was mid-August, and school would start again on Monday. Now, they had to squeeze every drop out of summer before it ended.

Their backpacks were stuffed with everything imaginable—nothing had been forgotten. The day before, Peter and Mikael had scoured the house and garage for anything they might need for their three-day adventure.

Together with Filip, they had made detailed lists: one for food and snacks, another for clothes and hygiene supplies, and a final one for survival gear. Tents, sleeping bags, and sleeping mats weren't included in their "brilliant" list system—they deemed those too obvious to mention.

The food and snacks list included items like hot dogs and buns, chocolate milk ("Pucko"), two loaves of sweet bread, rocket cheese, chips, and, finally, a candy bag filled with ten-cent "rabbit droppings."

The list had been much longer when the twins handed it to their mom before she went shopping. After crossing out nearly half the unhealthiest items, she told them, "This will have to do. If you're hungry, you can always come back home."

The twins' best friend, Filip, went by the nickname "Fille." He had spent a lot of time coming up with nicknames for the twins in return. For Mikael, he had tried at least five different ones but eventually gave up and just called him "Micke." One of the less successful suggestions…

Cast aside into the trash bin along with other less successful alternatives was Misse. It simply didn't sit well with either Peter or Mikael. Coming up with a nickname for Peter had been much harder, and he had eventually given up altogether.

Filip was almost a head taller than the twins. For a while, he had been called Big Fille, but eventually, it had just become Fille. Probably because saying Big Fille took twice as long as just Fille, and also because they lived up north in Sweden, where shorter words were generally preferred.

The boys lived in a small community called Timmerlunda, and even though the town was small, it had a large catchment area and could easily fill an entire school with classes up to ninth grade without any trouble. The school was called Stenäng school, the same school where they had just completed their first six years.

The following week, they would begin seventh grade, which also meant moving into new facilities in the larger building. The primary and middle grades were housed in the older building, the one that had always been there and previously accommodated all classes. But as the community grew and more families moved in, the single building became too cramped, causing an expansion. The new section was completed five years ago and has since housed the upper grades. Soon, it was time for Peter, Mikael, and Filip to venture into these new premises.

As they continued their journey into uncharted territory, they passed the lake where, earlier that summer, the boys had launched Agda, their homemade raft. Filip's dad had helped with the materials and framework because he didn't trust the boys' construction skills and wanted to ensure the raft would be seaworthy. The name Agda came from one of their neighbor's hens, and they had already decided beforehand that a watercraft should have a woman's name.

The lake was simply called the Lake. It probably had an official name, but locally, it was just The Lake. It wasn't particularly large, only a few hundred meters long and about half as wide. It was also where they skated in the winter and where their teacher had once fallen through the ice one winter.

She had been very thorough in checking the ice before allowing the students to step on it. She had even sent the school's custodian to evaluate the ice's thickness. Before letting the students out, she explained the dangers: reeds, the pier, the point, the inlet, and the outlet. But what she had missed was the channel, and it was at just such a spot that she fell in herself.

Everything happened very quickly. The children heard her calling for help, and when they looked in her direction, they saw only her head and shoulders sticking out above the ice.

At first, they were completely paralyzed. She kept shouting, and her words became louder and more frequent, peppered with forbidden words. That's when the children snapped out of their paralysis. They found a long branch to extend to her, and after much effort, she managed to grab it. They pulled with all their might and eventually succeeded in rescuing her from the hole.

She was deeply embarrassed by the mishap and had a hard time admitting she had overlooked a danger. It was also the last time she took any students skating on the lake.

When the trio reached the end of the gravel road, it turned into something more akin to a tractor path. Normally, parts of the path would be filled with water, but it hadn't rained in over a month, and the forest was very dry. This allowed the children to continue walking side by side, though with Fille in the middle at the highest point of the path, the twins looked even shorter.

"Hello there, my little dwarfs," said Filip, placing his hands on the twins' heads.

Peter and Mikael laughed so hard that their stomachs ached, and they had to lie down. While lying there, they decided to rest for a bit. When Filip felt his stomach rumble, he suggested they have something to eat.

Peter and Mikael pulled out double sandwiches from their lunch bags and started devouring them. Filip reached into his backpack and rummaged around for a while. Finally, he pulled out a gigantic apple he had carefully picked from one of the family's many apple trees.

The twins stared at the apple for a long time, and then Peter said in amazement, "What do you fertilize your trees with, anyway?"

"I don't know…" Filip replied, holding the apple up in front of him, "...but on Saturdays, Dad usually stands by the trees to pee out the beer he's drunk. Apparently, it's good to fertilize with beer."

Filip's dad didn't drink beer, only on Saturdays. It usually started on Thursday, and sometimes he called in sick on Friday so he could keep drinking straight through to Saturday night. After that, he slept all Sunday to recover from work the following week. He was never angry or threatened. He mostly wandered around the yard, fixing one thing or another, but Filip's mom didn't like it at all. She had threatened to leave him, but every time he straightened himself out, and eventually, she dropped it. It was thanks to his kindness that she stayed with him; otherwise, she probably would have left him long ago.

Filip loved his dad more than anything else. He never said no when Filip asked for help with something but would quickly jump to his feet and follow Filip, no matter what it was.

"How much farther do you think we have left?" Filip asked, taking a big bite of the apple and thinking back to when they had stood on top of that hill a few days ago, which marked the center of the village park, and decided to walk all the way to the horizon. It had started as a joke, but the more they thought about it, the more they wanted to do it.

***

The three boys wanted a grand, dignified end to their summer break, as Filip had called it, and sat down at the top of the hill to brainstorm ideas. But since they had already done almost everything that three twelve-year-old boys could do during a summer break, Mikael had finally just blurted something out. They had initially laughed about it, but after all three of them let the idea settle a bit in their heads, they looked at each other and said in unison: "Let's do it."

The view ahead on the horizon mostly consisted of forests, but there were also plenty of mountains. Almost immediately, the boys started planning, and the excitement grew to become almost unbearable. They wanted to leave as soon as possible. "Let's go," Peter had said, jumping to his feet, eager to hurry home to start packing.

"No time to waste," Filip added, rolling over like in a somersault before landing on his feet. Mikael just screamed with joy and was the first to reach the bikes, which lay in a pile at the foot of the hill. They raced home on their bikes, and as usual, it was Filip who first skidded into Småkulle street with a broad drift to mark that he owned it.

Filip only lived two houses away from the twins, but the distance was more than three hundred meters. In the house between them lived an elderly man who was at least one hundred years old. His name was Tore. The three had decided to sit down in Mikael and Peter's Garden to start planning the mighty journey. As the boys flopped onto the couch on the porch, the twins' mom sat inside the kitchen reading a notice in the local newspaper.

The teenage girl who had been reported to be missing nearly a month ago has still not been found. Police and volunteers have searched large areas in and around Timmerlunda without finding any trace of the missing girl.

The police told Timmerlunda newspaper that they receive similar cases every year, and the children almost always come back home eventually, that the teenager ran away from home and then regretted it.

"We hope that's the case this time, too," the police officer concluded.

Mikael, who had now finished thinking about Filip's question 'how much farther it was,' held up four fingers in the air and answered: "Maybe three hours."

"You're crazy," Filip chuckled back, jumping over Mikael with the apple firmly gripped between his front teeth.

"You can't show four fingers and mean three, you weirdo." Filip and Mikael wrestled around for a while in the lingonberry bushes, but after a while, they got tired and lay down on their backs to rest. After a moment, Peter said: "I wonder what the overfed brothers have done during the summer; we haven't seen them at all."

"Think they've gone to their summer house by the sea," Filip replied, tossing the apple core toward a tree.

"Good thing we don't have to deal with those jerks," Mikael said.

The overfed brothers had gotten their nickname because they always looked exactly like that—stuffed full. A little chubby, but not exactly fat, like two big milk cartons. And something else that was a little funny was their first names: Lue and Mayst. Their dad worked as a developer for a company that made glue and paste. I wonder what they were thinking when they named their kids.

The brothers liked to fight, especially with the twins Peter and Mikael. Luckily, they had Filip, and over the past year, when Filip had grown a lot both in height and width, the overfed brothers had finally given up fighting with them.

The last time the overfed brothers had fought with the twins, Filip had surprised them by sneaking up from behind and slamming their heads together so hard that stars and birds had appeared above their heads. Mikael had said afterward that he was absolutely sure he had heard birds chirping when they left the brothers to their fate after walking away from the scene.

"Well, what do you say? Should we keep going so we can make it there sometime?" Filip said, standing up.

Peter and Mikael agreed. They put on their backpacks and continued along the tractor path. The clock was approaching eleven, and the heat was really starting to set in. It had been hot all summer, but by the weekend, it was supposed to be extremely hot—up to 28 or 30 degrees.

A nice way to end the summer, the three of them had thought when they read the forecast in Timmerlunda newspaper. But now, as the heat took hold and the sweat was dripping from them, all three prayed to God that there had to be a lake or stream further along where they could cool off.

After an hour of trudging through the dry forest, the boys heard something that sounded like rushing water. They dropped their backpacks and hurried toward the sound. And just as they had hoped, it was a stream winding its way between rocks and trees, and a little further ahead, they could see that the stream became wider and calmed down a bit in its flow.

A perfect swimming spot. Clothes flew off one by one. They hadn't brought any swimming trunks, but none of them cared. As is typical at that age, it could be a little embarrassing to be naked in front of others, but with your best friends, it was no problem. Even though they joked with each other:

"You need a sugar cube if you're going to manage to bring out the little one," or: "Are you turning into a girl or something?"

All three knew it was just for fun, and none of them was better or worse than the other at making comments. First, it was Mikael who accidentally tripped in with his underwear still around his ankles. Then came Filip, and last was Peter.

"So nice," Mikael screamed as he threw his underwear onto a rock.

"And warm for a stream," Filip said.

"I wonder where the water comes from," Peter said.

"It looks really clean, though." Mikael tasted the water and made a face. "Yuck. It tastes like mud. Definitely not from any spring."

"You fool. Don't drink the water, silly," Peter chuckled, splashing water toward Mikael. Then it started. There was a full water fight between the three, but after just a few minutes, they were completely exhausted and decided on a ceasefire. All three declared themselves winners of the match.

After a short rest in the stream's calm, they each sat on a rock to dry off in the sun. Mikael wrung the water from his underwear and neatly placed them on a rock in the sunlight. From the spot, they could now see how the forest gave way to more lowland terrain, and a bit further ahead, the mountains they had aimed for came into view. Now, it couldn't be far, they thought—max two hours, and then they would be there.

"Shall we grill sausages when we get there?" Peter asked.

"Do you think we can make it until then, or should we eat before?" Mikael asked, looking really hungry.

"I think we should wait until we're there to eat. That way, it'll motivate us," Filip suggested, and Peter agreed.

Mikael stuck out his tongue in its full length to show that he was hungry.

"What, are you Gene Simmons now?" Filip asked, standing up and starting to play the air guitar.

"Oh, we should have brought a cassette player so we could have played some Kiss," Mikael sighed, looking completely defeated that he hadn't thought of the idea before they left.

"Okay, and who would have carried it then?" Filip said. "Not me, that's for sure. It's already enough trouble with the backpack."

The boys decided to drop the thought of the cassette player since they didn't have it with them, and who would have carried it was irrelevant. If they had thought of it earlier before setting off, maybe they would have decided not to bring it anyway. It was quite big and heavy.

After drying off in the warm sun, they put on their shorts, T-shirts, and shoes and set off again along the now almost nonexistent trail. The tractor tracks had ceased some time ago, and the path they were walking on now mostly resembled an animal trail. They found it hard to believe that other people had walked here before, but after an hour, they spotted an empty beer can.

After a couple of hundred meters, they found two more. Someone or some people had definitely been here before. They wondered who it might have been but figured it was probably some teenagers who had come out here earlier in the summer to party, far away from watchful parents and neighbors.

Neither the twins nor Filip had ever considered trying out mid-strength beer. It was enough to see the older ones down by the lake on weekends to discourage them from the idea. One evening, when the boys had sneaked around a bit farther away, they had seen one after another of the older kids on all fours, throwing up straight into the lake.

As mentioned, that had been enough to change their minds.

The forest ended, and they began their ascent up the slope of the mountain. After following the trail for a while, they turned around to admire the view. Now, they could see just how far they had actually come.

Far, far away, they saw the tower of Timmerlunda Church, and if they really squinted, they could even see the horizon line of the sea many tens of miles away. Or maybe it was just wishful thinking. But they had walked far, and the clock was now approaching six in the evening.

After a short while of walking, they found the perfect spot to set up camp. Next to a protective rocky outcrop, there was a small grassy area where the tent could fit.

"This will be perfect," they called out in unison.

Mikael at once started looking for kindling so he could make a fire. His stomach was now completely empty, and he was seriously worried that he might starve to death.

Filip and Peter were eager to get the tent up, and when the last stake was hammered into the ground, they smelled Mikael's first grilled sausage. He was sitting, shaking, with the sausage in his hand, chewing frantically when Filip and Peter sat down next to him.

"You'll survive. You can relax, Micke," Filip said reassuringly, putting his arm around Mikael. "I've read that you can survive without food for three weeks. It's worse without water, though; you can only last three days."

The boys grilled the whole pack of sausages, and afterward, they decided to explore the area. As mentioned, it was a perfect spot to camp—the grassy patch where the tent fits and the rocky outcrop nearby that blocked any potential wind from the north. But right now, it was almost completely still.

On the other side of the rocky outcrop, the mountain continued upward for a bit, maybe fifty meters in elevation. The boys decided to go all the way to the top, and when Filip set his foot on the highest point, he said, "Today's biggest achievement is now complete. Behold the view, gentlemen."

"Wow, what a view. What do you think we see over there in the distance, the chimneys spewing white smoke?" Mikael said, cupping his hands around his eyes like binoculars.

"I think it must be the paper mill in Bofnäs. It's at least in the right direction," Peter answered, thinking at the same time: that's not a place I'd want to work when I grow up. But it was exactly there that he would later take a job when he couldn't finish his studies.

The boys stayed at the top for a long time, and as the sun began to sink lower and lower in the sky, they slowly made their way back to camp. When they sat down next to the now extinguished fire, Mikael suddenly noticed something hanging out from the rock wall beside them.

"Look," he said. "What is that?"

Peter and Filip also spotted it and quickly stood up to walk over to the stone wall.

"It looks like a piece of a scarf or something," Filip said as he grabbed the fabric and tried to pull it loose. The fabric was stuck firmly in the rock, as if it had fused with it.

"Damn, that's tricky," Mikael said. "How can something like that just happen?"

The boys pondered the piece of fabric for a long time, trying to figure out what had happened. But they couldn't make sense of it. The fabric, which they had now agreed was a scarf, had indeed fused with the rock.

"Fille, you're the smartest of the three of us. Can you explain this to me before I go crazy?" Mikael said. But both Filip and Peter stood there like two question marks, unable to utter a word. They eventually decided to think about it more the next day and went to bed instead.

As they lay there, silent in their sleeping bags inside the tent, Filip suddenly said, "One." Mikael thought for a moment about what was going on, but when Peter said "two," Mikael understood and added "three." They continued like that until they reached a thousand, and before they knew it, all three had fallen asleep. Mikael had already given up at two hundred.

Outside the tent, it was completely quiet; the weak wind from earlier had completely died down, and the only sounds were the boys' calm breathing. Three little boys dreaming back on all the fun they had during the summer vacation, but now it was almost over. Three best friends who would soon be reduced to just two.

In the middle of the night, Mikael woke up after dreaming about the scarf on the rock wall. In the dream, he had stood in front of the rock wall trying to pull the scarf loose, and suddenly, the entire mountain had collapsed on top of him.

He listened to see if either of the others had woken up, but their breathing was calm and steady. And now, as he lay awake there, the half-liter of water he had drunk before going to bed reminded him, and he decided it was best to crawl out of the tent before an accident happened. Quite annoying for a twelve-year-old.

When he stepped out of the tent, he walked a little beyond the mountain ridge, and while he stood there emptying his bladder, he took the opportunity to admire the amazing starry sky.

So far from the disturbing city lights, the stars appeared incredibly clear, and in a thick band across the sky, the inner parts of the Milky Way shone brightly. But he also noticed that something was wrong with the sky, that the black wasn't quite black, but purple. Never had he seen such a night sky.

Even though he was dead tired and needed to go back to the tent to continue sleeping, he couldn't tear his eyes away from the amazing view. He stood there for a long time, thinking about what an incredible end to the summer vacation it was.

Ten weeks were soon coming to an end, and it felt like an eternity had passed since the bell had rung that last day at school. Now, he hoped it would never end, and he remembered the day when the school had rung out for the last time when they had run down the stone steps at the main entrance of Stenäng school.

Chapter 2

Peter turned away from the window. With the memory of Mikael's last summer vacation still in his mind, he gently raised his right hand to his cheek to wipe away a tear. He picked up the letter from the table and, with wet eyes, read the text once more. This time, he was able to understand the content of the letter while also thinking about the scarf that had been missing from the mountain ridge that morning when he and Filip had stepped out of the tent.

"An opening in the mountain," he read, thinking back on how strange it had been with that scarf. The night before, it had been firmly attached to the mountain, and by morning, it was completely gone!

Scarves fixed to mountains don't just disappear. Does Mikael mean he vanished with the scarf?

Questions began piling up in Peter's mind, but he didn't expect any answers.

Maybe I should get in touch with Fille?

The last time Peter had contacted Filip was two years ago. Peter had been out partying and felt lonely when he came home and drunkenly called Filip. The response had been that Peter needed to pull himself together, and after that, Filip had hung up.

Ever since Mikael's disappearance, Peter had been a different person, and within a couple of years, things had gone terribly wrong between him and Filip. For several months, weekend after weekend, Peter had partied hard and been mostly unpleasant to everyone, especially Filip. He had tried to make him understand: "Enough is enough! If you don't stop, you can forget about me as your friend," and Peter had responded, "You don't understand anything; go to hell, you idiot!" before slapping him in the face. Filip had just walked away and decided to completely sever ties with Peter, something he had kept ever since.

Peter had long since put it behind him and now wished nothing more than that Filip had done the same. Now, he needed Filip more than ever.

Peter grabbed his phone and dialed the number, held the receiver to his ear, and waited. After a few rings, he heard Filip's voice in the other end and at once felt a calm return to him.

"Hey Filip, it's Peter. Please don't hang up!"

After a long pause, Filip quietly and briefly responded, "Hey."

"I got a letter from Micke."

"Are you drunk?"

"No, I'm not drunk, and I have the letter right here in front of me. I'm sure it's Micke who wrote it. We need to meet, Fille. As soon as possible."

"Hello. It's been ten years since Micke disappeared. Why would a letter from him come now?"

"I don't know! And I agree that it seems really strange, but I feel it's Micke who wrote this letter. It's his handwriting. And what's also odd is the paper the letter is written on—you must see it to understand. When can we meet?"

"Do you still live in the one-bedroom flat?"

"Yeah."

"Okay. I'll be at your place in an hour," Filip responded and hung up.

Peter exhaled and felt incredibly relieved that Filip was on his way. He decided to clean up before the visit and started by clearing the coffee table of beer cans, then tackled the rest of the apartment. Afterward, he took a much-needed shower.

Peter had just managed to fill the coffee maker when the doorbell rang. He hurried to the hallway and quickly ran his hand through his damp hair as he passed the mirror.

When he saw Filip standing at the door, he couldn't hold back the tears. Seeing Filip again after so long, and at the same time knowing that Mikael was no longer with them, made him feel very weak.

Filip stepped toward him and said, "What the hell," then gave him a tight hug. He whispered, "How are you really doing?"

"You don't understand how much I miss Micke."

"I miss him too, you know. Show me the letter now."

Filip kicked off his shoes and sat down on the couch as Peter filled two large cups of coffee. After setting the cups on the table, he pulled out the letter and handed it to Filip.

After Filip had read through the letter a couple of times, he looked at Peter and said, "It's Micke who wrote it. I recognize his handwriting and all the misspellings. I remember from school that he always had trouble with whether there should be one or two consonants in a row. Do you remember?"

"Can I see? I must have missed that."

Peter grabbed the letter and now saw that he had overlooked it earlier.

"Doesn't the paper feel strange? It feels wet even though it isn't."

"Can I feel it?" Filip asked, reaching for the paper.

He felt it between his fingers, and just as Peter had said, it felt damp and moist, but when he took his fingers away, they were completely dry. He lifted the letter and held it up to the light from the window and could clearly see that this paper wasn't made by any machine. This paper was handmade.

"And then there's the envelope. It's a regular standard envelope but with one of those forwarding labels stuck on it. And if you flip the letter over, there's our old address, also written by Micke."

"I wonder what he means by: You'll know when you see the opening in the mountain?" Filip said, finishing his coffee.

"Hmm. I've been thinking about that, too. And at the same time, I've been thinking about that scarf that was missing in the morning, the one that was stuck in the mountain. It must be the mountain wall Micke means. Don't you think?"

"Yeah. I can't think of anything else. But the thing is: You'll know when you see the opening in the mountain. What kind of opening? There wasn't any opening in the mountain, was there?"

"There's only one way to find out. We must go there, at least I do. Are you coming with me?" Peter said, urging Filip, looking deep into his eyes.

"Of course I will," Filip said without hesitation. "You, me, and Micke, you know."

"God, it's good to hear that. Thanks, Fille," Peter said, pulling Filip in and feeling the tears return.

Just a few days later, Peter and Filip walked down the same gravel road out of Timmerlunda that they had taken many times before. But this time, as adults. Still, they could feel how that feeling started to creep back when they were twelve years old, how their legs began to tingle, and how the sense of excitement returned. Both understood that Mikael was missing to complete the trio, but it still felt pretty good. Perhaps they were on their way to him now.

Peter had told his colleagues at work that he needed to take his vacation right away and explained that it was crucial that it was approved. Since the production at the factory usually slowed down a bit during the summer, there was no problem.

For Filip, however, who had gotten a job in the military after completing his national service, it had been harder. He had been scheduled for guard duty all summer and wasn't supposed to get any vacation until August. But he had eventually managed to convince a colleague to cover for him during his first week. Filip had told him that he hoped a week would be enough, but he might go over by a couple of days.

"Max one and a half weeks, then it's on you," had been the response. Filip had promised, but it turned out that wasn't enough time. He would need coverage for much longer than that.

After just a few hundred meters, they arrived at the lake. They stopped when they heard the sounds of children playing, and Filip asked Peter if he remembered the raft.

Peter replied, "Of course," and they both began to recall that wonderfully warm summer by the lake, where the grand Agda had been built with the help of Filip's beer-drinking father, Oskar.

***

"Come on now, boys," Oskar urged the children as the materials for the raft were hauled on a cart toward the lake. The cart was filled with planks and nails, ropes and straps, four large blocks of polystyrene, and somewhere at the bottom of the cart, a few beer bottles rolled back and forth, occasionally making a clinking sound. Filip's father,

Oskar, had promised to help the boys with the raft, but he wanted to bring a couple of beers down to the lake. These few had turned out to be six. On the way to the lake, they saw a few teenagers ahead of them. They also seemed to have beer's with them, as evidenced by their walking style and the beer cans scattered here and there in the ditch.

One of the teenagers, named Pernilla, would later become the first missing person in the Timmerlunda municipality that summer. When the cart was parked on the grass by the dock, the children jumped into the lake to cool off. Oskar sat down with a beer to rest after the effort with the cart. It was Saturday afternoon, and the heat was increasing by the minute.

The summer had been extremely hot, and there seemed to be no end in sight. It hadn't rained a drop since the end of May, and it was already early July. If it didn't rain soon, the farmers would have a tough time; the fields were already quite dry, and the crops were growing poorly.

A few more weeks without rain and the harvest would be ruined. After the boys finished swimming, they ran up to Oskar and said: "Now we need to get started." The children were eager to finish Agda and could hardly wait. In the days before, they had sat on the twins' porch and made a drawing of how the raft should look. With homemade juice in hand and freshly baked buns on the table, they used a pencil and a ruler to design the most amazing raft ever constructed.

Afterward, they reviewed the drawing and realized they would need help to build it. It had become that complex. Filip ran home to ask his dad, and after half an hour, he returned with the good news that Oskar had gladly accepted the responsibility. That same day, they began gathering materials for the raft. There were plenty of planks and nails both at the twin's house and at Filip's farm. They had begged their surely two-hundred-year-old neighbor for some rope, but when it came to the polystyrene blocks, they ran into a problem. They had cycled all around Timmerlunda without finding a single piece of polystyrene and had finally given up. But when they sat on the grass outside Filip's house in the evening, Oskar came out and asked why they looked so sad. The children explained the problem of finding sufficiently large polystyrene blocks to make Agda seaworthy. Filip's father sat quietly for a long time, muttering to himself, then went back inside the house. The next day, when the children met after breakfast, four GIGANTIC polystyrene blocks were sitting on Filip's garage driveway.

The children stood frozen, thinking a miracle had occurred. But in reality, it was just Oskar who had woken up really early and driven with his car and trailer to the coast, where he knew there was a company that made storage boxes from polystyrene for fish. He had bought four large blocks and driven back home before the boys had even woken up. Now, he stood behind the curtains in the living room, smiling widely as he watched the boys outside, looking like three exclamation marks. Later that evening, Agda was ready.

A creation three meters by four, with a trampoline on one end, or perhaps the bow. On the long sides, two oars were attached to brackets, and at the other end, the stern, there was a sunshade so the sailors on the raft could have some shade if they wanted. Now, they stood at each corner, waiting for the signal from Filip's dad.

When he counted to three, they all pulled with all their might and pushed with everything they had. Even though Oskar had only used his right hand while his left hand was occupied holding the beer bottle, they managed to get Agda into the water relatively easily. And how beautifully she floated! "Wow," the boys shouted in unison. They were ecstatic.

Agda lay perfectly flat in the water, just low enough to make it easy to climb up onto the deck. And imagine the boys' surprise when Oskar was the first to dive into the water.

"Come on now, boys," he shouted to the boys.

"Who's the first to get on the raft?" The boys threw themselves into the water and scrambled up onto the raft. Filip and Peter began to row, and Oskar lay under the sunshade. Mikael lay flat on his stomach at the very end of the trampoline, smiling as he looked down at the water. What a joy.

The sun had just set, and the sky began to slowly turn a beautiful red. And if you looked closely into the red, you could see shades of dark purple. Mikael, who was lying and looking down at the bottom of the lake, saw how it also glowed in dark, dark purple, but it was nothing he reflected on directly at that moment. However, it did catch the attention of the thirteen-year-old girl, Pernilla, who had passed by the lake earlier in the day.

****

Pernilla, who was now standing in front of the rock outcrop beyond the forest, was slowly, slowly being drawn into the illuminated rock wall. She wore a multi-colored scarf loosely around her neck.

Pernilla was somewhat of a loner but would hang out with her friends sometimes when her mother insisted: "Come on now, Pernilla. Go with them now that they're here asking for you." And that was exactly what happened that morning when some of her classmates wanted to take her on an exploration into the forest. Karin, Bosse, and Hasse were somewhat of the class troublemakers, something Pernilla's mother had no idea about. She was just happy that they had come to ask for her. Pernilla had reluctantly agreed to go.

They had taken her past the lake and continued along the gravel road toward the forest and the heights beyond. They had tried to cheer her up, made her talk a little, asked questions, and kept at it, but it was all in vain. Bosse had brought a backpack full of beer, and they planned to get Pernilla to drink a couple of them. When they reached the end of the gravel road and continued onto the tractor track, Bosse had pulled out a beer and offered one to Pernilla.

"After this, the shell might start talking a bit," he had said, followed by a loud laugh.

Pernilla had recoiled and shaken her head to show: "I don't want that at all." But after some persistent persuasion from the three, she had finally accepted it.

During their continued journey toward the mountain peak, they had managed to get her to drink three whole 50cl 4.5% beers.

By the time they reached the foot of the peak, Pernilla was thoroughly drunk. She had experienced that the first time a thirteen-year-old drinks alcohol, it doesn't take much to almost knock them out. And at that moment, when the world was spinning around her, the three friends had decided to leave her.

An hour later, Pernilla was standing alone in front of the illuminated rock wall, thinking she had hallucinated.

Peter remembered that wonderful evening on the lake. The water was probably close to thirty degrees, and it had been completely windless. No gnats or mosquitoes where they lay completely still out on the lake, with Filip's dad snoring in the background. And yes, it had been a completely beautiful sky, too, from what he remembered, a bit like the one they had above them now, but not quite as powerful.

"Shall we continue?" Filip said, waking Peter from his thoughts.

"Yeah, I guess it's time," Peter replied slowly, groggily.

Peter and Filip threw on their backpacks and continued along the gravel road. It was a nice summer evening, reminding them a bit of the summer ten years ago. So far, it has been really warm, and the forecast showed no changes. And just the other day, Peter had heard on the TV that they had been talking about unusually strong solar activities. American NASA reported that measurements from one of their weather satellites had hit a record high the previous week and that they predicted continued high solar activities going forward.

"How have you been lately?" Filip asked.

Even though it had been a long time since they met, Filip had never completely let go of Peter. The incident from school had since long been forgiven, and every time Peter had reached out drunk, he preferred to forget. Now, he wanted to look forward, make up for the years they had missed together, and maybe find Mikael again, no matter how crazy it seemed. He wasn't sure yet if he had decided to believe in the letter, but it did seem to add up: Mikael's handwriting, the misspellings, their old address. Yeah, maybe.

"Okay," Peter answered and looked up at Filip. "A lot of beer."

"Man, you have to stop with that, Peter. Otherwise, you'll end up like your dad."

"What? What do you mean? What have I missed?"

"First, he lost his job. Then he lost mom and the house, and now he lives in a rundown apartment in one of the rental buildings in Timmerlunda."

"That's crazy. Oskar, who was so kind."

"It's not always enough to be kind; you have to take care of yourself, too. Especially your job. I don't know what he's living off now. Maybe social benefits. It's been years since I visited him."

"I'm fine. As long as we find Micke, it'll work out. Man, I've missed him; you have no idea. Maybe it's hard for anyone else to really understand what happens when your twin brother disappears. I don't think you can put yourself in my shoes."

"Maybe not in your way, but I miss him too. Just like I've missed you. Damn, we were supposed to be friends for life. Don't you remember?"

"Yeah," Peter replied, starting to laugh lightly, and Filip easily joined in.

Now they had reached the end of the gravel road and started looking for the tractor track they had continued their journey at that time ten years ago. It wasn't easy to find, but eventually, they could make out the outlines in the vegetation. They picked up speed along the track, and just like back then, it was bone dry in the forest. The lingonberry bushes cracked under their feet as they walked, triggering the memory of "The Great Forest Fire" they had accidentally started during one of their amazing barbecue evenings that summer. It was during one of their bike trips that Mikael had managed the feat of gathering the fire brigades from three municipalities into one forest.

Peter and Filip continued along the tractor track and began approaching the dam where they had stopped to cool off together with Mikael. The vegetation had grown thick here too, but it was still open enough for the sun's rays to reach and warm the water.

"Shall we?" said Peter.

Filip, who was completely soaked with sweat by this point, threw off his backpack and started taking off his clothes without responding.

After cooling off in the refreshing water, they sat down to dry off on the same rock as ten years ago. And just like back then, they let their gazes rest on the mountains a bit further away and sat in silence for a long time.

The sun was warming up quite a bit, and after a while, Peter asked, "So, how's it working in the defense?"

"Well, it's actually alright. But they're cutting back so much. It's like the politicians think the threat from the Russians has suddenly just disappeared. Sure, a lot is happening over there in the East; soon, the whole bloc will probably fall apart as it seems, but just because of that, they can't just shut down the whole defense."

"That's crazy about Olof Palme too."

"Mm. It was probably the Russians behind that, if you ask me."

"You think so?"

"Ah, I don't really believe in anything. But maybe. By the way, have you heard about the high solar activity that everyone's talking about?"

"Yeah, a little. I heard something about being able to see the northern lights quite far south if you're lucky and that this week would be the peak."

"Isn't it cool? We should keep an eye on it. It's apparently pretty rare. The last time there was such high activity was around ten years ago, but back then, they didn't know much about it. Now, apparently, NASA has a satellite that can measure it."

"We'll have to stay awake late tonight. If we're lucky, maybe we'll catch a glimpse of it. How far do you think we are from the mountains now?"

"Haha, maybe an hour," said Filip, holding up two fingers and nudging Peter into the water.

They swam for a while longer and then continued their journey toward the campsite near the mountain.

Later in the evening, after they had set up the tent, they sat down and made a fire. Peter remembered when Mikael had been so terribly hungry and stuffed down sausage after sausage.

I wonder how he's doing; he thought and closed his eyes.

He was now completely sure that Mikael was alive; he could feel it in his whole body, just like a twin could feel. And now, as he was at the place where Mikael had disappeared, the feeling became even stronger.

There's something about this place; he thought as he lifted his face toward the night sky and opened his eyes.

Above him, he could see that the sky had taken on a slightly different hue, a bit towards purple, and he recalled that the night after Mikael had disappeared, the night sky had had the same color.

Then he thought back to the morning when he and Filip had woken up, and Mikael's sleeping bag was empty.

***

"Fille, wake up," said Peter, shaking him in his sleeping bag. "I think Micke is up and maybe already fixing breakfast."

"I'll be there in a minute," said Filip, who wanted to lie and rest for a while.

It was still early in the morning, but the sun had already risen quite a bit in the sky. Inside the tent, the heat had risen significantly, and Peter felt how nice and cool it was when he stepped out of the tent.

"You're going to die from heat if you stay in there," Peter shouted into the tent after stepping outside.

When he stood up and let his gaze pan around, he couldn't see Mikael anywhere, and he suddenly felt a big lump in his stomach. Maybe he already knew, subconsciously, that his twin brother was missing. It was not something he reflected on then and there. He didn't understand why he had that feeling in his stomach at that moment.

He walked around for a while, looking up past the hill and back again. When he didn't see Mikael anywhere, he started calling for him.

"Quiet, I want to sleep a little longer," came the reply from the tent.

"You need to get up and help me look for Micke," Peter called back, now becoming more and more worried. "I can't find him, and he doesn't answer when I call."

Suddenly, it flashed into Peter's mind. The scarf! When he had passed the hill earlier, something felt wrong, and now he remembered what it was. It was the scarf. Yesterday, it had been stuck in the rock face, and now it was gone!

He quickly turned around and looked at the rock's face, and he was right. He hurried over and started looking for it but couldn't find it anywhere.

It was truly gone.

He shouted to Filip that the scarf was missing, which made him react. Filip flew out of the tent in nothing but his underwear.

"What! What did you say? Is it gone?"

"Yeah, totally gone."

"What are those tracks in front of the rock wall?" Filip asked, crouching down and tracing the tracks with his hand. "Maybe some animal came by last night and managed to get the scarf loose."

"I don't think so; there's not a single trace of the scarf left. If an animal had managed to get it loose, there would still be something left, in case it had torn it up, I mean. But now, there's absolutely nothing from it. Totally gone."

"You might be right. But where has it gone then?"

"Forget about it for now; we need to find Micke."

Peter and Filip searched all morning without finding a trace of Mikael. They circled the mountain, went up the other side, and down again. They searched in the forest, calling his name, but no Mikael appeared.

As the afternoon approached, they decided to head home to tell their parents what had happened. The twins' mother became furious with Peter for not keeping an eye on his brother, and after a while, it turned into pure panic.

She had felt it rise within her body. First, her legs began to shake, and she had to sit down. After that, it started swirling in her stomach, and she felt nauseous. As the icing on the cake, a sudden headache that felt like her head was about to explode. But in the midst of all this, she also thought of the girl who had gone missing earlier that summer, and how it had seemed like a one-time incident back then. But now, another child had gone missing, and this time, it was her child. Mikael.

Their father alerted the police, and search teams were dispatched. The military and volunteers thoroughly searched the area for several days, and a helicopter with a thermal camera circled the area. The police searched with the help of dogs, but the dogs behaved very strangely.

As soon as they entered the area where Mikael had disappeared, the dogs ran around in circles and couldn't pick up any scent at all. It was as if something disturbed them, something confused them or made them lose the trail. After a week, the search was called off without Mikael being found.

Peter and Filip were like two zombies; they felt neither alive nor dead, and the twins' parents were completely devastated. They refused to accept that Mikael was missing and tried until the last moment to get the search team to continue. They themselves had searched for him from early morning until late evening every day, but after three weeks, they too had to give up.

Mikael was truly gone.

They had asked the police if they saw any connection between Mikael's disappearance and the teenage girl who had gone missing earlier that summer and received the answer that the area where both had disappeared matched, but there were no further leads to follow. The police also mentioned that they had investigated the nearby properties but couldn't suspect anyone.

For the police, it was a mystery. But what the police had missed in the search for the girl was the scarf that had been stuck to the rock face. And just like in the search for Mikael, the dogs had again failed to pick up any scent and had mostly just run around aimlessly without any success.

"No, what do you say, should we go to bed?" asked Filip, giving a yawn.

"Not me, but you can go to bed if you want. It was at night that Micke disappeared, which means if something shows up, it should happen at night, I think."

"We can take turns if you want. Wake me up when you can't stay awake any longer, and we'll switch," suggested Filip, and Peter agreed.

Filip went to bed, and Peter wondered whether he should throw another log on the fire. He didn't want it to burn too hot, just a little. He didn't want the light from the fire to disturb his night vision, as he was afraid, he might miss something. He lay down on his back and looked up at the same night sky Mikael had seen the night he disappeared. Peter could also see the inner parts of the Milky Way, just like Mikael had, but also the purple light that Peter now understood was from the high solar activities. Mikael had also seen that light the night he disappeared, but unlike his twin brother, he hadn't understood that it was due to the high solar activities. That connection was not something a twelve-year-old boy would have known.

Peter managed to stay awake until the first rays of the sun started to turn the sky dark red. He had kept an eye on the rock face all night, and all night, it had remained just a normal dark rock face. Peter gave up around five o'clock and managed to crawl into his sleeping bag without waking Filip.

When Peter woke up, it was already eleven o'clock, and Filip had been up since seven.

"Good morning, sunshine," Filip said when Peter came out of the tent. Filip was sitting in the sun, sweating from the heat. The temperature had risen to nearly thirty, and later in the afternoon, it would get even hotter.

"Good morning."

"Did anything happen last night, did you see anything special? How long were you actually up?"

"I think it was five when I went to bed, and absolutely nothing happened. But still, I couldn't take my eyes off the mountain."

"It was only the first night after all; we'll have to keep an eye on it. I can take the first shift tonight if you want.

Eat something now, and then we'll go to the river to swim. If we stay here, we'll die of heatstroke," Filip said, tossing the cooler with food to Peter.

Peter made a couple of sandwiches, and then they walked along the trail to the river to cool off. The cooler went along since they planned to stay at the dam all day— it was way too hot for anything else. On the way back later in the day, Filip asked Peter if he remembered all the crazy things they'd done that summer.

"Do you remember the mobilization depot?"

"My God. How crazy we were," Peter said, tapping his head with his finger.

***

It was halfway through the summer break, and the boys had cycled off early in the morning to explore the land south of Timmerlunda. Seemingly, it was mostly wasteland, but there were also quite a few gravel roads crisscrossing the landscape.

They cycled for hours, and the strength in their legs seemed endless. One gravel road after another, intersections to the right and left, up and down, but the boys still seemed to know exactly how to find their way back home when the time came.

Suddenly, they came upon a large red wooden building with a flat black metal roof, somewhat discreetly hidden in the forest.

There was nothing showing what kind of building it was, but on the doors of the building, there were large yellow signs saying: "UNAUTHORIZED PERSONNEL KEEP OUT."

That very text made the boys want to explore what was hidden inside.

They placed their bikes behind the wooden building and began walking around it. At one gable, they saw a ladder hidden under a pile of boards. Mikael guessed that it had been used previously to get up onto the roof, so that's exactly what the boys did.

Once on top, they could see that there was a hatch, and with the help of a screwdriver from Filip's bike repair kit, they managed to unscrew the hinges of the hatch.

"Oh shit," said Mikael as he looked through the roof hatch. "Military stuff!"

"Let me see," said Peter, pushing Mikael aside. What he saw were three large military trucks and rows of shelves stacked with boxes.

"Get the ladder, Fille, so we can come down." Filip hurried to get the ladder, and when they managed to get it down through the hatch, he said, "Maybe it's best if someone stays up here and keeps watch in case anyone comes."

"I don't think either Micke or I can manage the first step down. It's too high for us. It might be best for both of us to stay up here and keep an eye out. You go down alone, Fille."

"Then you need to be quiet and really keep a lookout. If you see anyone coming, warn me in time so I can get back up."

"Of course," said Mikael, giving a thumbs up.

Filip took a step down, barely reaching the first rung of the ladder. He continued downward on shaky legs, a little afraid he might slip or step wrong, but after a minute, he was down.

"What do you see?" whispered Peter down the hole. "Boxes everywhere. And each stack is labeled with what it contains." Filip read aloud what was written on the signs: Pants, field shirt, motorcycle pants, coat... All the boxes were marked with some kind of model number: M50, M60... He guessed it had something to do with the year. He wandered around down there for a while, checking out the boxes one by one, and when he came across a box labeled "SCARVES," he tore it open and pulled out three of them. He then continued to the next part of the warehouse and found it held canned food and other items. Up on the roof, the twins were arguing about who should look through the hatch and who should keep watch for anyone coming. After a while, neither of them was keeping an eye on the outside or through the hatch.

A near full-blown fight broke out on the roof while Filip, unaware, continued his exploration inside the mobilization depot. He had managed to find a personal gear bag, which he now began to fill with various canned goods. And chocolate bars! Chocolate bars in abundance!

When he was satisfied, he decided it was time to head back up and whispered up toward the hatch: "Is the coast clear?" When he got no response, he shouted a little louder: "IS THE COAST CLEAR!" Still no answer, but now he heard stomping and noise from the roof and understood that the twins were busy with something else, it seemed. He slung the bag's shoulder straps over his shoulders and walked up to the ladder. He followed the steep ladder with his eyes, took a deep breath, and began climbing carefully.

When his head appeared above the roof, he saw the twins wrestling a short distance away. He called quietly to them, "What the hell are you doing? You were supposed to be keeping watch. Help out here now." They stopped fighting and walked sulkily back to the hatch.

"Peter is impossible to reason with," Mikael said, throwing him an angry look. "It was you who started it; you were supposed to take the first watch," Peter retorted angrily. "Forget it now," Filip said, throwing off the bag. "I've gathered a bunch of great things here, but we'll talk about that later. Now we need to get the ladder up and screw the hatchback on." Filip swung down through the hatch with his arms outstretched and managed to pull up the ladder a bit.

Then the twins helped, and they succeeded in getting the ladder back up without too much trouble. Peter and Mikael made up. When the hatch was back in place and the ladder tucked under the pile of planks, they rushed off. They headed toward their secret gathering spot just outside town, a little way into a forest where they had built a shelter between two giant boulders.

Once there, Filip opened the bag and pulled out a chocolate bar. "Here's the reward," he said, tearing off the wrapper and stuffing a piece into his mouth.

"So good," said the twins in unison, now friends again.

"What else did you get?" Peter asked with his mouth full of chocolate. Filip turned the bag upside down. Out rolled lots of chocolate bars mixed with cans of pea soup, meat sauce, meatballs, and sausage. There were also a couple of packages of cereal, and Mikael wondered what Filip had been thinking. But then they spotted the green military scarves. "One each," said Filip.

"I thought they could be our joint garments this summer to show we belong together. Kind of like gang gear, I thought." They wrapped the thin, comfortable scarves around their necks and tied a knot at the back. "Nice," said Filip. "But what are we going to say we got them from?" Mikael asked.

"We can't bring them home yet. We'll have to leave them here every night, together with the others, and only wear them during the day," said Filip, stuffing the last piece of the chocolate bar into his mouth and then opening another one.

Peter and Filip walked silently the last bit back to the tent by the hill. They were both tired after the long hike to the dam and then back the same way. It had been nice to spend the warm day by the water, but now when the clock was approaching six in the evening, it was still incredibly hot, and after just a couple of hundred meters on the challenging trail back, they were both dripping with sweat again.

After a calm and quiet evening, they decided to keep each other company into the night, until one of them got tired. They sat together beside the tent, admiring the fantastic night sky, which now shone an even stronger purple than it had the night before. Hours passed, and every now and then, they glanced over at the hill next to them, a hill that continued to be just an ordinary hill.

Chapter 3

Mikael woke up by the second mountain ridge and saw that morning had arrived.

Now, as he looked out over the field in front of him, he realized that some sort of grain was being grown here. A very peculiar kind of grain. Just a thick stalk with a solitary large ear hanging at the top.

As he followed the field with his eyes, he could see that a forest began a little further ahead, and at the boundary between the forest and the field, there was a gravel road. But what most caught Mikael's attention was the sky, or rather, what was in the sky.

A gigantic red sun was rising over the horizon, at least five times larger than the sun Mikael was used to seeing. It almost felt like it could be touched.

Mikael became scared. He shook with fear, and when he tried to stand up, his legs gave way, and he had to sit down again. He wanted to get to the gravel road but couldn't bring himself to even try.

With a lump in his throat, he turned toward the mountain wall, and using it for support; he finally managed to get to his feet. He could feel his legs becoming steadier, and eventually, he dared to let go completely. He thought and tried to figure out what had happened. He remembered how he had been sucked into the mountain wall at the campsite and then ended up here.

He thought: A parallel world and realized that there could be no other explanation for the mystery.

I must have ended up in another world!

He decided to explore the area and then return to the mountain when it started to get dark, hoping to get back to his world again.

He picked up the scarf from the ground and began walking through the strange grain field. From time to time, he let his gaze wander to the amazing yet frightening sun.

It was almost possible to look straight into it, unlike at home, where your eyes are blinded immediately. Here, you could also see the corona of the sun and how flames were cast out and then drawn back in.

Before he reached the road, he grabbed an ear of one of the stalks and pulled it off. He removed the outer layer from the plum-sized interior and took a cautious bite. It tasted good.

The flavor was a mix of nuts and bread, and he decided to gather a few. With his hands full of ears, he was reminded that he was only wearing underwear. He had put his hands where pants pockets would normally be but stopped when he looked down and made the dreadful discovery. Instead, he placed the ears in the scarf and carried it like a bag.

What if someone sees me like this? What will I do?

He understood there was nothing to be done about it; he just had to try to brush it off. What's so strange about walking around in underwear when it's this warm? He thought and decided to continue along the road, not thinking about it anymore. If he was lucky, he might find clothes somewhere along the road, maybe on a clothesline by someone's house.

If there are houses here at all? Maybe there aren't any people here, he thought, becoming scared again.

But a road, at least. Maybe …

He followed the winding road ahead and ate the freshly picked ears. He noticed that they filled him up but also that they made his mouth very dry, and he started to feel thirsty. He stopped and tried to listen if he could hear the sound of running water. He thought he heard something bubbling but wasn't sure. If it was water, the sound seemed to be coming from further ahead along the road.

He quickened his pace and almost started jogging. Occasionally, he stopped to listen, and the sound grew louder and louder until, finally, he saw a brook rushing by.

He hurried to the brook running along the road, squatted down, and drank from it using his hands. The water was incredibly good, the best water he had ever drunk. He drank until he could drink no more and lay down to rest for a while. He looked up at the trees, which reminded him of the spruce forest back home. These trees had thicker needles, but otherwise, they were quite similar, except for the size of the cones. Here, they were enormous, almost like coconuts.

Better watch out so I don't get one in the head, he thought and immediately got up and returned to the road. He now felt better, now that he was full, and his thirst quenched.

Typical Micke, Peter would have said. As long as he gets food in him, everything's peachy.

He smiled a little as he thought about his brother and how special he was to him. He was sure he could get back to his world again. If it was possible to come here, it should work the other way too. And think how cool it will be when

I get back and tell you about this place, he thought as he continued on the gravel road. But it would turn out to be harder to get back than he could have ever imagined.

Somewhere far off on the horizon, he saw smoke rising into the sky, and he understood that it must be coming from a house or at least from someone who was burning something. It was far too far to see clearly, but what else could it be? He estimated the distance to be, at most, an hour and looked up at the sun to estimate how much of the day was left. To his surprise, he saw that the sun had only just risen a little in the sky, even though it felt like it should already be late afternoon.

Are the days longer here? He thought and stopped to think. Sure, that could be it, why not? Everything has been different here compared to home so far. Actually, it's only the water that looks the same.

Along the road, there were more fields with ears of grain, and there was no shortage of water either. And after an estimated hour, he clearly saw where the smoke was coming from, and it wasn't from a house. It looked more like some sort of hut, though a well-built one.

The closer he got, the more details he could make out. He saw that it was made up of several parts: a larger section in the middle and two smaller ones on the sides. It seemed to be made of some sort of clay, and here and there, wooden sticks were sticking out.

A small path led up to the hut, which was located near a pond, and behind the hut, the mountain rose tens of meters. A small chimney stuck out from the main building where white smoke was billowing. When he reached the smaller path, he was only about a hundred meters from the building. He stopped and wondered if he dared to continue.

How will the person inside react? He thought. Here comes a little underwear boy walking all alone. What if they're hostile?

He started slowly walking toward the house, his bare feet dragging in the gravel. What he didn't know was that two red eyes were watching him from one of the openings in the wall. Eyes belonging to a heavily built creature with a mouth full of sharp teeth. Mikael continued forward toward the hut.

Earlier that night, a young girl had woken up by the same mountain wall that Mikael had ended up beside.

Nauseous and still dizzy from the three classmates' prank, she had wandered along the same path Mikael was now walking. Just as amazed as he was at where she was and just as taken by all the impressions from the new world: the trees, the purple sky that had taken over the light from the descending giant sun, the ears of grain growing in the fields lining the road, the good water. She had experienced all the same things Mikael was now experiencing. But the end of her night had been completely different from his.

When the dark purple sky had taken over everything, she had looked for a place to lie down and sleep. It had felt like the night would never end, but she hadn't gotten tired until now. She had tried to count how many times she had eaten the ears during the time she had wandered around the new world and figured it had been more than fifteen times. With that calculation, she guessed the night had lasted at least a full day in the timekeeping that applied back home.

She had made a bed from grass from the field and lay down to sleep when she heard a growling sound from the forest. She had become terrified and almost screamed loudly but managed to stifle the scream. Instead, she stood up and prepared to climb the tree near her sleeping place but didn't have time to put the plan into action before she felt two powerful, hairy arms around her.

What she had first thought was an animal, perhaps a wild boar or something similar, turned out to be a creature walking upright, like a human. The scream she had let out that evening could be heard miles away, but no one was there to hear it. The only beings in the area that night were the teenage girl Pernilla from Timmerlunda, who had, on a warm dark night with a dark purple sky above her, been sucked into the mountain wall deep in the forest at home and a strong, bestial creature with a breath that stank of death and decay.

Mikael continued down the road. When he was almost there, he veered left and began walking toward the side of the hut. Why he chose to veer left, he didn't know, but that maneuver probably saved his life that day.

When he reached the back of the hut, he was horrified to see a girl trapped in a cage a little further away. He immediately understood that he had to be careful, that there was an evil person here who was keeping a girl captive. He crouched down and whispered softly, hoping the message would reach the girl: "Hi, who are you?"

The girl turned around and saw Mikael.

With wide, startled eyes, she said: "Help me, please!"

Mikael started cautiously walking toward the cage, but then he heard a door open at the back of the hut. The squeaking hinges grew louder.

"Hide!" said the girl and curled up in the cage.

Mikael quickly looked around to see if there was any cover, but it was already too late. Out of the door came a large, powerful creature with hair on its back and arms and a skirt-like garment on the lower half. It stopped and turned its evil eyes on him.

Mikael panicked a little and turned to run. The creature followed with a gurgling roar and quickly closed the distance.

Mikael understood that he had to come up with a way to get rid of the creature, and without thinking directly, he aimed toward the mountain wall that ran along the back. Now, the creature was only about ten meters behind him.

He continued running through the tall grass toward the mountain and tried to see if there was any way to climb up quickly. He spotted a crack running diagonally up the wall and decided to try to climb there, hoping the creature wouldn't be able to follow. When he reached it, the creature was only five meters behind him.

Mikael kept going, took a leap toward a rock in front of him, and miraculously managed to grab onto a protruding ledge. Quickly, he got a foothold with his feet and began to scramble up the diagonal crack.

The creature stopped and reached up with its hands in an attempt to catch him but failed. Mikael had already climbed far enough to be out of the creature's reach.

Mikael continued upwards and could see that there were definitely more than five meters left until he reached the summit. The creature made a few attempts to climb, but unlike Mikael's agile body and small feet, the creature was too clumsy to be a good mountain climber.

When Mikael was almost at the top, he looked down for the first time. The creature was crouched at the bottom, looking up at him, opening its mouth, and making a gurgling sound that could scare anyone half to death.

But not Mikael. He now realized he had the upper hand and knew that he could escape from the creature again if necessary.

He continued the last bit of the climb and lay down to rest. He looked down a couple of times to see if the creature was still there. He could see it walking around down below, eyes focused on the summit.

Mikael began to come up with a plan to get the girl out of the cage and away from the terrifying creature.

Pernilla slowly appeared from her curled position and cautiously looked up after hearing the door to the hut slam shut. She lay still for a while, completely motionless, to make sure the creature was no longer outside. She had gone inward and shut out all the horrors when the creature chased the boy. She didn't know if the boy had made it, but she sincerely hoped he had. No one else knew she was here, trapped and locked in a cage, waiting to possibly be killed and eaten by the disgusting, hairy monster.

The boy was her only hope.

Suddenly, she heard a sound.

Pop!

And again.

Pop!

It sounded a bit like when rain starts, with large drops hitting the ground. She looked up at the sky but saw that there were no clouds, only a clear, bluish-purple sky.

The sound came again, and this time, it was right next to her.

She saw a small stone roll away from her. She looked up again, and out of the corner of her eye, she saw something moving.

It was the boy!

He was standing at the very top of the mountain, waving his arms to catch her attention.

Thank God, he's alive, she thought, unable to hold back the tears.

She smiled at the boy and waved her hand to show she had seen him. She also saw that he was trying to communicate with her. First, he tilted his head, leaning on his hands, then pointed at himself and then at her. She at once understood what he meant: he would come down and rescue her when night fell. Pernilla nodded up and down to show she understood.

She had noticed that there was no lock on the cage; the only thing resembling a lock was a thick chain threaded several times through hooks attached to the door and the cage wall. The ends of the chain were threaded over an iron spike hammered into the ground just outside the door. If only the boy could get down unseen, she could easily explain it to him when he was close enough.

The boy waved at her, held his gaze for a moment, and then disappeared from the summit.

Pernilla looked at the sun and saw that it hadn't moved much since the last time she checked, which was long before the boy had arrived. It was still at the same height. She began to understand how slowly time passed here— that one day could feel like several days in her reckoning.

Would she have to wait long before being rescued?

It felt like anything could happen before that time came—she might even be dead and eaten by then. The fear returned, and the brief moment of joy when she had seen the boy at the top of the mountain was gone. Now, she was back in hell again.

Mikael thought he recognized the girl in the cage. He was almost certain he had seen her before, back home in Timmerlunda. It must be the missing girl from seventh grade, he thought, trying to remember what she might have been called. Annika… Pia…

After meeting the girl, he had slowly gone into the forest, away from the mountain wall. Now, he was on his way out of the forest again.

He continued along the edge of the forest, too afraid to step into the open field, worried there might be more of the same creatures. Outside the forest edge was a meadow with low grass and flowers in scattered clumps.

On the other side of the meadow, there was a gravel road. Whether it was the same road he had walked on before, he didn't know, but he assumed it could be. If it was, it must have gone around the forest he had just crossed through. He thought he couldn't stray too far; he needed to be back when the sun went down to try and get the girl out of the cage, but also to get back to the mountain wall at the cornfield in time to return to his own world again. And hopefully, with the girl. That was at least his plan.

The day felt incredibly long. Just the time spent crossing the forest felt like at least five or six hours, and from this morning until now, it felt like at least an entire day had passed. He squinted at the sun to try to figure out what time it was and was surprised to see the sun still so low in the sky as if it were still morning.

Besides, it had been a long time since he had eaten anything. He was starving; it felt like there was a vacuum in his stomach. At least he had managed to drink water. He had crossed several streams with flowing water, so he was fine on that front. What had Filip said? That you could survive three weeks without food!

"Bullshit," he caught himself saying aloud. "That doesn't apply to me!" he continued, not caring that he was talking to himself.

He hadn't seen any more fields with the good, filling ears of grain for a while and wondered if he should turn back. But that would mean he'd have to pass through the creature's territory. If he kept going forward instead, and considering how much time was left in the day, he'd have plenty of time to find something to eat but still get back in time before it got dark. He decided to keep going. At the same time, he spotted something that looked like a horse-drawn cart at a summit on the other side of the meadow.

He stood behind a tree and peered cautiously forward.

On the cart sat a man and a woman. From a distance, they looked like two completely normal people, except their clothes looked very old. The man wore a black pointed hat with a wide brim and something that looked like a long white dress. The woman, who had long, light hair, was dressed in a gray dress and also wore a hat of some sort. The cart was pulled by something that at least resembled a horse, though Mikael couldn't quite figure out what was off about it. He thought the neck looked far too short, and he couldn't see any tail. Otherwise, it was quite similar to a horse, at least the kind Mikael was used to.

He thought the people looked kind, but he didn't quite trust them. He thought, maybe if I follow them for a while, I'll get the courage to approach them. He continued in the same direction as the couple but had to increase his pace to keep up.

After about an hour, the road approached the edge of the forest, and Mikael considered revealing himself. Maybe he could get some food from the couple if they had any. If his stomach had felt like a vacuum earlier, he could never find the right word to describe how it felt now, no matter how much he tried. That's how hungry he was.

He decided to take the chance.

Pernilla walked around inside the cage. The cage wasn't big, but she felt she had to move. Three steps in one direction and three steps in the other. She had to keep her head low so she wouldn't hit the tin roof. She was glad for the roof, not because of the risk of rain but because it shielded her from the sun.

She had water, and there was no shortage of it. A large barrel stood outside the cage, and a hose with a valve was connected to it. She could drink from it whenever she needed.

Periodically, the creature came out with food for her. It was mostly stalks from the fields but also some fruits she had never seen before. They were completely unknown to her but tasty.

One thought had crossed her mind: that the creature's intention was to fatten her up to then have a proper feast. Why else would it keep her captive and feed her so much? But after the boy had been there and shown that he would come back to rescue her, she tried not to think too much about it. The only thing she focused on now was not to remain still. She had to keep moving and stay in shape so she could quickly run away once the boy managed to open the door to the cage. That was what she tried to fill her thoughts with—freedom and returning home.

Maybe the boy had been here before, and maybe he knew how to get back. That was at least what she hoped.

Mikael was about ten meters ahead of the cart when he stepped onto the road. The horse reared up and became frightened, but when it calmed down a bit, he saw the man stand up with a rifle aimed at him.

Mikael had seen many Western films in recent years and reacted instantly. Both his hands shot up into the air to show that he wasn't a threat.

The man shouted something Mikael didn't understand, and then the woman took charge and pushed the rifle aside with her hand. The man looked at her in surprise for a brief moment but then turned his attention back to Mikael.

She rummaged inside the cart and picked something up in her arms, jumped down from the cart, and began walking toward Mikael. The man stayed where he was, still ready with the rifle in his hand, as the woman slowly approached Mikael. She looked him over from head to toe and held out a blanket to drape over him.

She must have been quite puzzled. A strange little boy, almost naked, suddenly stepped onto the road. Strange in such a way that he didn't quite look like a normal boy. To her, he seemed a bit misshapen—his nose was positioned too high, and the distance between his eyes was far too short. He had small feet and a strange garment in the middle of his body. A little garment with tiny figures drawn on it.

She grabbed Mikael's arms and lowered them, then wrapped the blanket around him and pressed a hat onto his head, sitting down on her haunch.

Mikael felt how heavy the blanket was as if it were made of lead. The hat also felt heavy.

The woman lifted her hand to Mikael's forehead, pushed his bangs aside from his eyes, and said something in a foreign language. He tried to show that he didn't understand by shrugging and shaking his head. The woman turned to the man and said something, then returned her gaze to Mikael.

Mikael gently raised his hand and touched his thumb to his index finger, bringing the hand to his mouth in a gesture to show he was hungry. The woman understood this language and took his hand, beginning to walk toward the cart.

She shouted something to the man, who was still standing, ready with the rifle. He shook his head and angrily laid down the rifle in front of him and turned toward the cart.

When Mikael and the woman reached the cart, the man handed something down to the woman, who then gave it to Mikael. It was a fruit of some kind, and he immediately began eating it. He thought it was delicious and devoured it eagerly. The woman smiled at him and let out a small laugh. It was the first time she had seen someone eat an entire fruit without peeling it first.

She helped him onto the cart and then sat on the bench. The man took the reins and made a noise that got the horse moving. The woman picked up another fruit from the box at the back but made sure to peel it before handing it to Mikael. Now Mikael understood why the woman had laughed at him earlier.

The journey continued along the gravel road, and occasionally, the woman gave Mikael another fruit. The man grunted something to her each time, but the woman snapped back, showing who was in charge.

Mikael sat inside the cart, which was filled with wooden boxes, more blankets and hats, and a strange mechanical thing with levers and knobs.

The roof of the cart was made of some sort of metal—thick and gray. He felt the blanket he had wrapped around himself and saw that it also had inserts made of the same type of metal as the roof, though in smaller pieces. Could it be lead? He thought. It certainly felt like it, and he recognized the texture from all the lead weights he had attached to fishing lines when they went fishing.

A couple of times, they turned off the original path, and Mikael tried to keep track of the intersections. He didn't want to get lost, as he knew he would need to find his way back later. He just hoped the couple didn't live too far away if they were indeed headed home.

After about an hour, Mikael saw a house at the end of the road, and when the man loosened the reins to let the horse choose the path, he understood that this was where they lived.

The horse stopped just outside the house, and the man and the woman disembarked from the cart. The man held tightly to his rifle, and the woman raised her hand toward Mikael in a gesture for him to stay in the cart. The man continued toward the house and disappeared around the back. After a minute, he came around the other side of the house and waved the woman over.

It was a small house. Only one story high and maybe five by five meters square. The walls and roof were covered in metal, the same kind as the cart's roof. Above the entrance door, there was an extended metal roof.

The woman took Mikael by the hand and hurried him inside the house. Mikael might not have been the sharpest kid in Timmerlunda, but he began to suspect that the people here were afraid of something. Why else would they walk around in these heavy, lead-lined clothes and build their houses with lead plates? After all, wasn't it built from lead? Wouldn't it have been easier to use regular fabric for the clothes, and there were plenty of trees to build houses with?

When they entered the house, the couple went into one of the rooms, and after a short while, they came out again and changed into clothes that Mikael was more familiar with. The woman also had clothes for Mikael, which she handed to him. He took off his heavy blanket and changed. It felt good to get rid of the weight and put on more normal clothes, even though they felt a little too large. The woman signaled Mikael to sit down on a chair.

He sat there, disoriented and lost. It was only now that he began to truly understand that something terrible had happened. The shock from everything he had gone through started to fade, and only now did he begin to realize that he had experienced something... indescribable.

First, waking up in a completely foreign world, walking around in areas that were completely unknown to him, encountering a creature he could only relate to comic books and horror films, a lone girl kept captive in a cage, and finally meeting two people who looked strange.

Tears came in abundance.

Chapter 4

Just as they were sitting there, Peter and Filip noticed a faint light at the bottom of the rock wall. Peter, who was almost dozing off, raised his left hand and checked the time on his pocket watch. It was already one in the morning.

The light spread from the ground in front and into the mountain. It was as if the light was eating its way into the mountain, dissolving it. Like lava but with a much stronger glow. At first, Peter thought he was seeing things, but when Filip suddenly shouted, "Look!" while pointing at the light and jumping to his feet, Peter realized that it was really happening.

The rock wall lit up, crackled, and emitted a strange flashing light. It bulged outward, and a circular glow moved toward Peter and Filip as they sat in front of the fire.

"It's happening," said Peter, quickly getting up and running toward the tent. He rummaged around for a moment and came back with both his and Filip's backpacks.

"Get ready now," he called out, dropped Filip's backpack, and then stood in front of the wall. Filip was completely stunned. He wasn't prepared for this. He never thought something like this could happen. He was only here for Peter's sake; he never believed the letter, never thought Mikael had actually reached out. He never thought this would happen. He just wanted to be with Peter again. Not jump into a glowing, crackling rock wall!

"Filip, what's wrong with you?" Peter shouted, staring at him intently. "I don't know. What's happening?"

The rock wall was now illuminated several meters up and continued to bulge outward more and more. Peter was ready to take the leap, feeling something pulling him, drawing him toward the mountain. "Come on, Filip, in a second. I'm jumping." Filip felt the ground tremble beneath him and realized he had to make a quick decision. He thought quickly of Mikael, how much he missed him, how much he missed the trio he, Peter, and Mikael had been.

All the adventures they had shared. How much he wanted to return to the time they spent together. That was all he wanted. The three of them again. He threw the backpack over his shoulder and shouted loudly, "Let's do this," following Peter as he stepped into the crackling, trembling, shimmering rock wall.

In a fraction of a second, they were sucked into the mountain and consumed by its interior.

They woke up in front of a different rock wall than the one they had just been pulled through. Just like Mikael had done ten years earlier, but in this world, only one day had passed since he crossed over. Lying on the brownish-green shimmering ground, looking up at the incredibly beautiful purple sky, they were just as surprised as Mikael had been by what they saw when they opened their eyes after the tumultuous transition from one world to another.

From a universe still in its infancy to another, billions of years into the future. To a world where the sun had grown enormous, where the radiation had wiped out most of the population. Where only those with the strongest genes and those who had managed to protect themselves from the deadly radiation had survived. Where mutated plants had appeared, managing to withstand the lethal dose they consumed daily in the form of free electrons sent out from the sun's corona. To an Earth whose interior had been drained of most of the iron that had once generated the magnetic protective field against the evil that now wanted to destroy whatever remained on the once beautiful, green planet where Peter, Filip, Mikael, and Pernilla were now located. None of this was known to them. Peter and Filip were completely unaware of where they had ended up. They saw the sky. They saw the tall grass with its single, hanging ear swaying above, and they saw the rock wall behind them. And they saw a large white sign with black text that said:

WELCOME TO MY PLACE

Peter stood up and walked toward the sign. He stood there for a long time, contemplating this creation that he understood had been made, set up, and written by Mikael, his twin brother. Filip stepped forward and laid his fingers on the text. He traced each letter, each word, and slowly and seriously said, "Mikael is here!" They looked at each other. Filip saw the tears leaving Peter's eyes, the tears that slowly streamed down his cheeks.

Peter stopped himself from wiping them away as he felt his own eyes begin to water. "I know," Peter said, "No one spells so terribly like Micke." He looked at Filip and laughed. They sat down, leaned against the rock wall, and after a while, fell asleep with their arms around each other. Several hours later, they woke up to the light of the sun, now beginning to show on the horizon. It was red, hot, and huge.

Only a small part of it showed, but the heat it radiated was incredibly intense and warm. They had now been in the parallel world for only a few hours. In the world back home, the year was nearly over. Six months had passed since they crossed over, and a nationwide alarm had been sent out only a few weeks after Filip's employer, the Defense, noticed he was missing.

Partly because they feared a foreign power might be behind his disappearance and partly because they suspected he had simply decided to abandon his duty and flee the field. Peter's employer at the paper mill in Bofsnäs, however, had simply grown tired of Peter never showing up after his vacation and had fired him remotely by sending a letter in the mail.

Filip jumped up, threw off his T-shirt, and began fanning himself with his arms. "Shit, it's hot." Peter grabbed his backpack and pulled out a Pucko. He opened it and drank half of it in one go.

"Pucko, you rascal," Filip said. "I know," Peter said, holding it in front of him.

"Wanted to experience a little nostalgia, I thought."

"Mm, ha, ha, ha. Reminds me of Micke and his excuse when we got back from Rågmanstorp. After, we drank vodka with Pucko, do you remember?"

The boys had cycled along the main road to Rågmanstorp to explore the ditches along the way. Suddenly, they discovered a plastic bag full of bottles. Mikael jumped off his bike while riding to be the first to open the bag.

When he pulled it up, he brought out a bottle of vodka. Peter, Filip, and Mikael looked at each other and thought for a moment. It wasn't beer and beer makes you sick. Vodka though! The bag also held some bottles of Pucko, and Mikael opened one at once.

As he began drinking the Pucko, Filip thought he should try it with the vodka. After an hour in the ditch, at least half of the bottle had been consumed by the boys. Then they saw the bus to Rågmanstorp coming towards them.

Three twelve-year-old friends, wearing denim jackets and green military scarves, headed towards Rågmanstorp, taking a chance with a bag of Pucko and a half-liter of vodka. Back came three incredibly drunk little brats, thrown into a social services minibus.

The staff knocked on the door of the Svensson family to hand over the little rascals, and Mikael's apology to the parents was: "Someone had poisoned the Pucko."

"Of course, I remember," said Peter, handing the Pucko over to Filip.

Filip drank the last of it and said, "Okay, what's happening now?"

Peter walked back to the sign. He had noticed something sticking out from the side. It was a rolled-up paper, the same type as the letter he had received. He unrolled it and saw that it was a map. A map that might lead to Mikael.

"A map," he said, looking at Filip.

"Can I see?"

Peter and Filip turned the map this way and that, studying it carefully, and concluded that it would take them at least ten or twelve hours to reach the place marked with an X. The place where Mikael was supposed to be. They also saw that there were a couple of spots along the way that they definitely had to avoid. These places were marked with skulls. The map also showed where there was water and fields with edible grains.

"I wonder what's at the places marked with skulls?" Filip asked.

"Mm. I wonder, too. We should probably be careful anyway."

On the back of the letter, it said that they had to put on the hats and dresses in the bag behind the sign and that it was of utmost importance. Peter lifted the bag with the clothes in it and noticed how heavy it was.

"Why do we have to wear this stuff? What are they made of, really?" he said, pulling the clothes out of the bag. "Maybe it has something to do with the sun," Filip said. "You can see how it looks, how close it seems. Maybe radiation?"

"Yeah, it looks like there are small lead plates sewn into the fabric for protection, maybe? We should probably wear them."

The friends changed, put on their backpacks, and started walking through the field. Filip picked an ear of grain to try. He thought it tasted good and gave the rest to Peter. At the gravel road, they turned right and continued along it for a couple of hours. Peter read the map and saw that they were now approaching the first skull-marked area.

"We need to step off the road now and walk in a circle around."

Filip grabbed the map to take a look. "Is that supposed to be a mountain?" he said, pointing at the map.

"Not the prettiest drawing, but I think so," Peter replied, lifting his gaze to look around.

In the distance, he saw something that looked like a mountain peak and said, "Maybe we should go around? It looks tall if that's what we're seeing over there."

He pointed at the peak he had spotted, and Filip agreed.

They entered the forest lining the road and began to make their way through the first tangled and wild section. They could feel the air getting more oxygen-rich, and the moisture in the vegetation soaked their clothes. After a couple of hundred meters, the path opened up a bit, and it became easier to move forward.

On their right side, they could glimpse the mountain peak through the treetops. They continued their trek through the forest, and both Peter and Filip cursed the heavy clothes. They were getting really sweaty, but they didn't dare take them off. Whatever kind of radiation it was, it seemed not to harm the plants at least, they thought.

After another hour or so of hiking through the forest, they reached a small pond. It was mostly surrounded by marshland, but at one end, they could see rocky cliffs. They set their sights on that end, and when they arrived, they decided to take a quick, refreshing dip. No more than a couple of minutes, they decided. It felt fantastic. It was warm and delightful, probably thirty degrees in the water.

A few minutes turned into a quarter of an hour, which turned into half an hour. It was wonderful and refreshing until something started slithering toward them in the water.

Filip saw it first. A giant serpent-like creature with front limbs like a crocodile was approaching them at an alarming speed.

"Out of the water!" he screamed loudly at Peter, who had just resurfaced after a short dip.

Filip, who was right at the edge of a rock, climbed out of the water at once. Peter, on the other hand, who hadn't yet realized the danger, was in the middle of the pond, far from safety.

"Hurry! There's a snake in the water. A big one! With front limbs!" Filip screamed hysterically.

Peter paddled toward Filip as fast as he could. Arms and legs flailing in the water in pure panic, and despite the seriousness of the situation, Filip could barely hold back laughter.

"Swim properly, you idiot!" he shouted at Peter.

Peter tried to yell back, but nothing he said was understandable. But despite his poor technique, he managed to reach the rock where Filip was standing just before the snake could catch up.

Filip reached for a thick branch that had fallen from a nearby tree and stood ready to strike the snake if it dared to come closer.

"Get up quickly. It's right behind you!" he yelled, extending his free hand. Peter grabbed Filip's hand and hauled himself up onto the rock just as the snake's jaw, filled with sharp teeth, snapped shut.

Filip released Peter, who barely found his balance at the last second.

Immediately afterward, Filip swung with all his might at the snake's head and landed a perfect hit right on top of the snake's skull.

The snake froze for a second and became completely limp.

Just as its lifeless body was about to flip over in the water, its enormous body jerked and turned back. For a brief moment, it lay there in the water, completely still, observing them. Then, it splashed and disappeared as quickly as it had come.

Peter and Filip sighed with relief.

It had been close—either Peter or both of them could have been in serious danger, and they realized that they needed to be more careful from now on. This time, they had been lucky, but next time, they might not be as fortunate. They quickly dried off in the sun and put on their dreadful dresses and hats again to continue their journey toward Mikael.

Chapter 5

Sitting on a chair at a kitchen table, crying with his hands in front of his face, was a small twelve-year-old boy, lost in a completely foreign world. Unaware that he was on a planet that had been waging a war for millions of years against a steadily growing star, their sun. Cities that had been destroyed by the strong radiation, which had slowly but surely eaten away the meager protection they once had. Cities that were now almost entirely erased, with only small, modest signs left to reveal that they had once existed.

The people who had managed to escape to the countryside to start a new primitive life had built their small houses from lead sheets, grown crops that thrived in the new climate, and were considered the winners in the war against the sun. People with strong internal defenses and the right genes had not been as affected by the radiation. But there was also evil. Terrible, monster-like creatures that hated humans. And with the lack of animals, they sought their flesh.

What Mikael did not know was that time behaved differently in this world. He understood, given how slowly the sun moved across the sky, that the days were very long, but what he didn't know was that aging also behaved differently here compared to his home world. For every day in this world, ten years passed in the Timmerlunda world, which could have disastrous consequences if he ever managed to get back.

The woman sat across from him at the table and sympathized with the boy. She had no children of her own and saw in the boy the child she had never had. The maternal feelings were there, and they had always been there.

A long life, longing for the child she had never had. She understood that the boy could not speak their language; perhaps the child couldn't even talk. She hadn't heard a single word from the boy yet and decided to try to get him to speak.

She took his hands and moved them away from his face, then said to him in her language, "Who are you? Where do you come from?"

Mikael opened his sad eyes and cried, "I don't understand what you're saying."

The woman smiled when she heard him speak. But she also grew concerned that he did not speak their language. She wondered how she could make herself understood, but Mikael beat her to it. He showed that he was holding a pen and pretended to draw on the table. The woman jumped up and searched for a pen and paper. She placed the paper in front of Mikael and handed him the pen.

Mikael had been thinking about the girl. He drew a cage with the girl inside. Then he drew the monster next to it and showed the drawing to the woman. He realized that he had forgotten something and grabbed the paper again. When he finished drawing, he handed the paper back to the woman.

She studied drawing. She understood most of it. First, the image of someone being held captive by a well, which was what the monster-like creatures were called. Then the second image, where the well was lying down and a person was taking the captive from the cage. She concluded that the boy wanted to rescue the captive and that it would happen when the well was asleep. But she didn't understand the round ring that the boy had drawn above the cage in the second picture. Mikael's intention was to show that it was night when the moon had risen in the sky. But this planet in this world didn't have a moon.

The woman nodded at Mikael to show that she understood. She called her husband over and told him about the boy's drawing. The man looked down at Mikael, said some angry words, and then went back into the other room. The woman hurried after him.

Mikael understood from the man's angry behavior that he didn't like the idea of rescuing the girl. But it didn't matter to Mikael, and he had already decided to rescue her, with or without their help. He had promised her.

He walked up to the small round window, which was no bigger than a plate, and looked outside. He could see the horse standing under the eaves of the entrance door, with a strong net around it, like a cage.

Probably as protection from the monster creatures, he thought. He squinted at the sun and felt that it hadn't moved much in the sky. He understood it would take a long time before he could rescue the girl.

But will she survive that long, he thought, feeling a worried sensation deep inside his stomach?

The woman came out from the inner room again and crouched down in front of Mikael. She nodded at him to show that she had convinced her husband to help. Mikael's face lit up, and he couldn't resist giving the woman a hug.

He held onto her, long and tight, and felt how the lump in his stomach disappeared, replaced by a feeling of safety, almost like hugging his own mother.

After a while, the woman gently pushed Mikael away and showed that she was going to cook. She made a fire in a stove and then lifted a hatch in the floor.

Under the hatch was a staircase that led down to a food storage area. She came up with a basket full of various fruits and vegetables and then cooked a stew that they ate at the table.

The man and the woman barely said a word during the meal, and Mikael understood that it was because of him. The man was probably upset because the woman had made him bring the boy to their home and then had convinced him to help rescue the girl.

After the meal, the man changed clothes and went out to the field to work. He had the rifle with him.

The woman sat down with Mikael and started drawing a picture on the paper that Mikael understood, showing the country where he had ended up. At the same time, as she pointed at Mikael, she moved the pen around on the picture. She wanted to know where he had come from.

Mikael shook his head and tried to think of a way to explain to her what had happened. He thought long and hard, then drew a planet with a small sun far away. After that, he drew a similar picture, but this time with a bigger sun closer.

Then he pointed to show that he came from the first planet and was now on the second. He then pointed at the girl in the cage and immediately after, back to his planet. He held up his hands with palms up and shook his head to show that he didn't understand how it had happened.

The woman pondered Mikael's drawing and his explanation, and she was completely confused. Could he really have come here from another planet? How could that have happened, she wondered.

Mikael took the pen again and drew a small mountain, a mountain that glowed and crackled, and a little stick figure beside it. Next to the figure, he wrote "Mikael." He tried to explain by pointing out that he came from the mountain. This made the woman even more confused. Mikael showed that he and the woman could reach the mountain after the sun went down and that he could then show her what had happened. The woman pointed to her mouth and then out toward her husband. Mikael assumed she was going to ask him first.

The woman put on her outer clothes and went out to the cart to bring in the wooden boxes of food. Mikael met her at the entrance door to help carry them the last bit. Then, they worked together to get the food down to the pantry under the house.

Mikael tried to pass the time by either dozing off on their wooden sofa or exploring everything that was inside the house. Most of what he could find seemed familiar, though the designs were still different from the things at home.

Cooking utensils like pots and frying pans seemed identical, but for many other things, he didn't understand what they were for, like a round wooden ball-like object with small holes in it. He decided that he would keep thinking about it until he figured out its function.

After several hours of thinking, without success, the man came back into the house. He hung the rifle above the door and stood looking at Mikael. He didn't look exactly angry, but neither did he look happy. Still, something positive, Mikael thought it was time for dinner again. The woman repeated the same dish as before, and Mikael ate it and found it delicious.

Afterward, they all sat around the table, and the woman took the courage to tell the man about Mikael's explanation of where he came from. She also showed him the drawings. The man just shook his head and gave both the woman and

Mikael a sideways glance, but the woman stood her ground, and in the end, the man agreed.

He pushed his chair back, got up from the table, and went to fetch the wooden ball with small holes in it, the very one Mikael had long since given up on trying to understand. He also brought small wooden pegs, which he began to fill the holes with. From time to time, he looked out toward the sun and held the wooden ball between himself and the sun.

After a long while, when he was satisfied with what he was doing, he took out paper and a pen. He drew a line at each edge to create two small columns on the sides and one large column in the middle. In the side columns, he drew a sun with a line over it, and in the middle column, a shining sun.

Then, he began filling the middle column with small lines, showing the time after the sun had risen while checking the wooden pegs in the wooden ball. Afterward, he sat leaning over the paper and counted. After a long time of thinking and grunting, he drew a long line from the left column to the right and placed an X about a third of the way in from the left. He pointed at the X, then at the sun, and showed Mikael.

Mikael was initially completely dizzy and understood nothing. But after a while, when the man managed to explain by showing where the sun was and where the X was on the line, Mikael understood. The man had figured out how much time was left in the day.

Mikael studied the man's calculation and saw that there was still a long time before the sun would set. He held up the wooden ball with the pegs in it and tried to understand how it worked but quickly gave up. He also thought about whether the girl could last that long. Maybe they would have to attempt a rescue before it got dark.

Mikael took out the drawing where he had shown the woman the girl, that they had to help free her. Now, he drew a shining sun above it and showed it to the man. The man grunted a couple of times, looked at the woman, and then back at Mikael.

Then he stood up and went into the inner room and came back with Mikael's outdoor clothes, handing them to him. He then began putting on his own. Mikael smiled while also feeling a bit scared.

Pernilla sat in the shadow under the roof. It had started to blow a little, and it was pleasantly breezy. She tried to pass the time by exploring the area outside the cage and spotted a large beetle wandering around. It was over ten centimeters long, had a black, greenish, shimmering armor shell, and a sturdy jaw. It had been walking in circles aimlessly, but suddenly it gained speed and headed toward a tin can set up with a small stick holding it upright a little further away.

When it reached the can, it stopped for a moment as if considering whether to go in or not. Suddenly, it gathered courage and continued inside. The stick fell away, and the beetle was trapped inside the can.

When the creature came out later, it had emptied the contents of the can directly into its mouth, chewed frantically for a while, and looked at Pernilla. It held out the can as if offering to share, but Pernilla just shook her head and grimaced badly. She thought she saw a grin from the creature.

Now, she looked up at the mountain, as she had so many times earlier in the day, hoping to see the boy. But just like before, when she had looked up, she saw no boy. She wondered if she could make it until nightfall.

Each time the creature had come out of its hut, she had been afraid that it would take her out of the cage to end her life. She only waited to see the creature slowly come toward her, circle the cage with its eyes fixed on her, see its razor-sharp jaws open, and watch the droplets fall from its mouth onto the dry ground outside the cage as small depth charges dropped from high above into a dry, dusty sea.

Now, as she sat there, she thought she heard a cracking sound from the road. She quickly twisted around to try to look around the corner of the hut. The road was partially obscured from her position, but she could see a little of it. And wasn't that a horse cart she spotted a little further away? Two people were sitting on the cart, and it was headed toward the hut. And as far as she could see, one of them was a boy.

Mikael and the man turned onto the small gravel road leading to the creature's hut. The man gestured to Mikael to be ready. Mikael lifted the heavy rifle, rested it on his weak shoulder, and aimed at the hut. He was a little afraid of accidentally hitting the girl, but as long as they were on this side of the hut, he felt fairly safe.

On the way to the creature's hut, Mikael had practiced a shot. It had made a loud bang, and a large bruise had quickly appeared. It hurt a lot, and the man had shown afterward that he needed to brace properly against his shoulder. Now, the pain had faded, and he wasn't afraid it would hurt anymore. He was also not too nervous about potentially having to kill a monster.

They neared the hut, and the man stopped a little before it. The horse veered right to eat from the grass at the side, giving Mikael a clear view ahead. The man stood up and shouted a couple of words toward the hut. Then he waited a moment and repeated the shout. They saw the door slowly open, and from the dark interior, something resembling a rifle appeared. The man shouted, and Mikael fired.

For a fraction of a second, a scene played in Mikael's head. How he had shot accurately with an air rifle at the summer fair that came to Timmerlunda every year. Peter and Filip had spent their one kronor without winning any prize, while Mikael had hit the bullseye with all five shots and won a giant stuffed animal. The other two had stood there gaping, wondering how it had happened.

"A natural talent," Filip had said.

"Beginner's luck," Peter had said.

The bullet from Mikael's rifle went straight through the door crack, and a moment later, a thud was heard from inside. The man touched his forehead and looked down at Mikael, who was massaging his now extremely sore shoulder. The door to the hut slowly opened, and as the light reached the darkness, they saw the creature lying flat on the floor.

The man took the rifle from Mikael, jumped off the cart, and walked toward the hut, ready with the rifle. He carefully looked inside, and when he turned to Mikael, he pointed with his finger where the bullet had hit, right between the eyes.

Pure luck, Mikael thought and sighed with relief.

Pernilla heard a shout. And another. Then, a loud bang followed by silence.

After a short while, she saw the boy come around the corner, walking toward her. She looked at him and couldn't hold back the tears.

He said to her, "Is your name Pernilla? I remember you from school. By the way, the monster is dead now."

"Yes, I'm Pernilla," she said, laughing through her tears.

Mikael looked at the gate to the cage and tried to figure out how to open it without Pernilla's help. When Pernilla came out of the cage, she gave Mikael a big hug.

"Thank you, my hero," she said and didn't want to let go of him. "Aren't you one of the twins in sixth grade?" she whispered.

"Yes, Mikael. My brother's name is Peter."

"I was afraid I would have to wait until tonight, which would have meant several days, it seems."

"Yes. Time really does go by slowly," Mikael said eagerly. "By the way, do you know where we are? I got pulled into a mountain in the middle of the night when we were camping, and suddenly I was here. Do you think it's a parallel world?"

Mikael surely had at least a hundred more questions, and he thought it was incredibly nice to finally talk to someone who understood him.

"I don't know. But were you beyond the lake when it happened?"

"Yes, far off by the horizon when you look from Timmerlunda. Far over there by the mountains, you know. Peter, Fille, and I were camping, and I went up in the middle of the night. And in the mountain, there was a scarf stuck that I tried to pull off. This one," he said, pulling out the scarf he'd brought with him in his lead suit.

"It's mine," said Pernilla, took it and held it against her face, then took a deep breath. She stood there for a long time, smelling the scarf. She recognized the scent from home and began to cry again.

Mikael stood still, watching her. He thought Pernilla was very sweet and considered comforting her, but didn't really know how. This was a situation he'd never been in before, and he had no idea how to behave. He wondered if he should go up to her and give her a hug like his mom would have if he were sad. Like even Peter would have done. But the thing was, Pernilla was at least half a head taller than him, and he thought it felt a little annoying. But he did it anyway.

He walked up and wrapped his arms around her, with his head pressed against her shoulder, and it felt really nice. In the midst of all the commotion, with the monster he'd just shot, with Pernilla, who had been trapped in a cage, being in a completely different world, far from home. All the things he'd been through which had shocked him, though he hadn't quite realized it until now. He couldn't stop the tears; they came in torrents.

They stood there for a long time, crying together, hugging and comforting each other. The man stood a little further away, watching them, and he couldn't stop the tears that slowly ran down his cheeks. Two little children, he thought.

The children they themselves had never had. He raised his gaze toward the sun and cursed it. He hated the damned sun that sent its cursed rays toward them. Why us? There were those who could still have children. He saw them every week when they went into the village, all the couples who could still have children. But not us.

Why not us?

As they walked back toward the cart, Mikael took a folded piece of paper out of his pocket and showed it to the man. He wanted them to continue to the mountain wall where he'd entered this mysterious world the night before. He first pointed to the drawing, then toward the mountain.

The man shook his head and pointed in the other direction. Homeward. Mikael wouldn't give up, though. He began pulling at the man's lead coat and moved toward the cart.

The man thought for a moment and decided it might not take that long after all. It would probably soon be over. The boy's exaggerated fantasy that he came from another world needed to be disproved. This was probably the only way. He raised his hands in a gesture of "Okay, okay. Fine then."

Mikael, Pernilla, and the man climbed onto the cart and set off from the creature's hut. They followed the gravel road past the fields of grain, slowly making their way to the spot where they had entered this world. From the safety of Timmerlunda to such a crazy place.

Mikael couldn't remember walking that far before reaching the creature's hut, probably because of the shock of waking up somewhere completely different, not at home. Now, they had traveled for hours.

The clouds gathered, and the temperature dropped as the wind picked up. Mikael was about to give up, but suddenly, he saw the mountain wall across the field.

"This is it," he said. At the same time, he felt raindrops begin to hit his face.

The man understood what he meant without knowing the language and stopped the horse.

They crossed the field toward the mountain as the rain intensified. Now, thunder rumbled in the background, and Mikael realized a storm was approaching.

They hurried the last bit, and just as they reached the mountain wall, lightning struck right beside them. The horse, which had stayed by the road, let out a frightened whinny, and the man turned to check that everything was okay with it.

When he saw that the horse was fine, he turned back toward Mikael and Pernilla, who had moved forward and stood in front of the mountain wall. Another lightning strike hit, this time directly above them, on top of the mountain.

At exactly the same moment, the mountain wall lit up in a glow, similar to what both Mikael and Pernilla had experienced before.

"Pernilla!" Mikael shouted. "Come on! The mountain is opening!"

Pernilla, seeing how the mountain wall lit up from the ground to the top, grabbed Mikael's hand and shouted, "Run!"

The man stood frozen a little further away, watching how the wall lit up in all its colors. The mountain wall crackled and made sounds and something like it he'd never experienced before. He wanted to reach out to grab the children but couldn't. He was terrified and didn't know what to do.

Mikael and Pernilla took a running start and threw themselves into the glow. And just as quickly, they bounced back.

"Again!" Mikael shouted.

They backed up a bit and started running toward the mountain, which now glowed even brighter. And once again, they bounced back and landed in a heap on the ground.

"What the hell," he said and took another run but soon realized it was completely hopeless. Just like the earlier attempts, he bounced back just as quickly. He sat down with his hands over his face. Pernilla sat down beside him and put an arm around him.

Mikael suddenly pushed her aside and picked up a stone he had spotted. He threw it with all his might at the wall and let out a furious roar at the same time.

The stone flew into the wall and disappeared.

"But," Mikael said, quickly standing up, "the stone could get through, but we can't."

"We don't have enough power and speed," Pernilla said, looking at him. "We need more speed."

She pulled Mikael a bit further from the rock wall and told him they would run on three. Once Pernilla finished counting, they gathered momentum once more.

The man stood and watched them as they rushed toward the mountain. He silently prayed that they would fail and smirked when he saw them bounce back from the mountain once again. Mikael sat still for a long while, staring ahead with an indifferent look, and then he started heading toward the cart.

Pernilla watched him and initially thought he had gone crazy and just wanted to leave. But after he had been up on the cart for a while, he returned to the mountain with a piece of paper in his hand. He tried to shield it from the rain as best he could and simultaneously searched for a suitably sized stone.

Sheltered from the rain, he tied the paper around the stone with a string and measured a throw at the mountain that still glowed and crackled. But it had weakened, and Mikael realized he needed to hurry.

He held the stone like a discus thrower and hurled it toward the opening in the mountain, and the stone disappeared into its interior. Immediately after, the light diminished in strength, and the mountain was just stone again. The clouds parted, and the sun's rays could once again start warming the ground around them. Pernilla walked up to Mikael, put her arm around him, and asked, "What did you put around the stone?

Mikael answered somewhat dejectedly, "A letter to Peter."

They sat down in front of the mountain, sad that they hadn't managed to get through. The man walked a bit along the edge of the forest to check on something he had noticed.

"I hope someone finds the letter," Mikael said.

"I think so. As long as it ended up where we came from. But we can't know for sure, can we?"

"Of course, it must have. Where else would it…?"

Mikael paused and jumped. "Do you mean it could end up in another world and not ours? If so, it would mean that if we had gotten through, maybe we would have ended up in another world too!"

"I'm just saying we don't know. We have no proof that it ended up in the right place. Right?"

"I still believe it ended up in the right place and that someone will find it. Then Peter will get it and come up with a good idea with Fille. And then they'll come and rescue us."

"I think so too," Pernilla said, now having put aside her earlier thoughts.

"And if they come here. Or rather, when they come here, they'll need lead clothes and hats. Did you see where the man went?"

"He disappeared around the bend over there," she said, pointing toward the forest edge.

"Stay here. I'll check the cart to see if there are more dresses. Call out if he comes," he said, hurrying off toward the cart.

Pernilla didn't like the situation Mikael had put her in. That she should keep an eye out while he just ran off and left her alone. If the man came, she'd have to explain why Mikael was inside the cart rummaging around. She decided to get back at him later. Because that's not how you treat a girl, she thought.

Mikael searched through the boxes and managed to find two sets of clothes. A bit too big, he thought, as he measured them against his body, but decided they would have to do. He pulled out another piece of paper and started drawing a map of the woman's and man's dwelling. He also thought he'd like to make a welcome sign with text on it since he was now certain Peter and Filip would succeed in getting through. He grabbed the top board from one of the boxes and started twisting and pulling it.

After a while, it started to come loose, and when he lifted the whole box and dropped it onto the cart floor, the board detached completely. He grabbed the pen and started writing a clever message in big letters.

When he was finished, he hurried back to the mountain again. He pressed the sign between two stones and placed the bag with clothes next to it. He rolled up the map and placed it behind the sign.

Meanwhile, Pernilla had been observing Mikael's energy. She had seen how he lit up when fixing the clothes and the sign. He proudly showed her the map, and she told him that it was perfect. Her anger over him leaving her with the responsibility as a watch had faded, and she wasn't as angry anymore.

When the man appeared from the forest, the children had just returned to the cart. They had no idea what he had been doing in the woods. As they began their journey back, Pernilla asked Mikael what he thought. When he answered, "He was probably in the woods taking a dump," she couldn't resist and burst into hysterical laughter.

***

Rune Erixson had been in the forest all day without any luck with hunting. He had hoped for at least a couple of hares, but on this day, it seemed like all the hares had gone into hibernation. At least they kept their distance from Rune.

His wilderness pants brushed against the low bushes, and a few thorns got caught in the fabric of the raspberry brambles as he rounded the mountain in a wide curve. He followed the edge of the forest and approached an open space in front of a rock wall. He adjusted the straps on his backpack that had started to slide down his narrow shoulders.

The jacket material was slippery, and he wished he had taken the thicker jacket instead, the one with coarser fabric. When he reached the open space, he took off his backpack,

110

unfolded the built-in sitting pad, and took out the thermos. He sat down and sighed.

Rune knew the forest around Timmerlunda like the back of his hand. It was part of the land he and the other hunters in the hunting team had leased for over twenty-five years, so he had made many trips there.

When he was alone in this part of the forest, he was often drawn to this spot. The beautiful view with the mountain peak behind it and the open, fine patch of land beside it.

As a child, he had often been here with his friends, and they would sometimes set up a tent and stay the night. He had always felt there was something magical about this place. He always got a special feeling in his body when he approached it, something inside him would wake up. Something that made him feel alive. But unlike Mikael, Pernilla, Peter, and Filip, he had never seen the mountain light up.

He poured himself a cup and sipped the warm coffee, set it down on the ground to pick up one of the incredibly delicious cinnamon buns his wife, Ingegärd, had baked. He took a big bite and reached for the cup again. Just as he grabbed the handle of the cup, he noticed a stone wrapped in a string. He let the cup stay and reached for the stone.

When he picked it up, he saw there was a piece of paper attached to it.

"This is strange," he thought, shoving the last piece of the bun in his mouth and starting to untangle the string. When he managed to free the paper, he unfolded it and saw there was text on it.

He read to himself, "I'm alive but can't get back. If you're reading this, please save me. Go to the campsite and wait for an opening in the mountains, you'll know when you see it. Micke."

His first thought was that it was probably just some kids playing a game. Even the bad spelling pointed to that. But when he turned the letter over and saw there was an address, he became a bit uncertain.

"Why be so serious otherwise?" he thought.

Rune folded the letter and stuffed it in his pocket, picked up another bun, and didn't think more about the letter that day.

A few days later, when Ingegärd was going to do a sixty-degree wash, she emptied the pockets of Rune's hunting pants. She laid the items on the washing machine and stuffed the pants into the machine along with the rest of the laundry. She turned the dial to sixty and pressed the start button. She then took Rune's things and went to him in the kitchen.

"I'll put your things in the hallway," she said curtly.

"No. Put them on the table, and I'll sort through them," said Rune, putting down the bolt of his moose rifle, which he was cleaning.

First, he picked up his snuff-box and shook it. Noticing it was empty, he set it aside. Then he spotted the folded letter.

"Ingegärd," he called out. "Come, look at what I found the other day."

Ingegärd, who had already reached halfway upstairs, turned around with a sigh. When she came down, Rune told her about the letter and let her read it. Ingegärd found it a bit odd but thought he should go and drop it in the mailbox at the address or even post it. She thought it might be a joke, and it would be fun to make sure the letter got delivered.

Rune agreed, and the next day he put the letter in a stamped envelope, wrote the address that was on the back of the letter, and dropped it in the mailbox outside the small service shop in the middle of Timmerlunda.

Mikael and Pernilla came back to the house, tired from the long trip back from the mountain. When the woman saw them approaching, she quickly went out to welcome them back. She looked at Pernilla for a long time and smiled at her. Now, they suddenly had two children to take care of, and she felt warm inside.

Mikael, Pernilla, and the woman went inside the house while the man stayed outside. Once inside, they took off their heavy clothes and sat down at the table.

Pernilla pressed her scarf to her face and took a deep breath. Then she said to Mikael, "I was wearing this the night I got pulled into the mountain. After I woke up, I saw the end of the scarf hanging on the rock wall. I tried to pull it off, but it wouldn't come loose. But I'm so glad you took it with you."

"Yeah, it was the scarf that got me here. If it hadn't been stuck in the rock wall, I probably never would have made it."

"I think it was meant to be. With the scarf, I mean, and that someone would find it."

"Maybe," said Mikael, pausing for a moment. Then he continued, "Do you think more could have come here to this world, or are we the only ones from our world, do you think?"

"I don't know. Maybe we're the only ones." The children sat for a long time, talking about what they had experienced. They also tried to come up with a way to get back. It had seemed impossible to get through the illuminated mountain. When they arrived here, they were sucked in, but getting back, in the other direction seemed much harder, maybe even impossible.

But the stone had disappeared, at least they had concluded. But they didn't know if it had made it all the way or even if it had ended up in Timmerlunda forest. It might have appeared in a completely different world. The woman sat next to them, trying to understand what they were talking about, but struggled to decipher their body language.

And the words coming out of their mouths were completely incomprehensible to her. She desperately wanted to be able to talk to them and wondered how that could happen. She had at least a thousand questions. She rummaged through an old schoolbook with pictures that she had once found in an abandoned house and placed them on the table. She showed it to the children and tried to explain that she wanted them to try to learn their language.

Mikael and Pernilla opened the book and immediately understood it was a textbook. There were pictures of all sorts of things, and next to them were symbols that looked very strange. The woman took the book and flipped it back to the first page, then pointed at a picture showing a woman. She then pronounced the word next to it.

The children tried to mimic her as best as they could, and when the woman was satisfied, she moved on to the next picture. They sat at the table for a long time, struggling with the words and trying to produce sounds they had never uttered before. Sometimes, they burst out laughing, and the woman couldn't help but laugh along.

The man came in after a few hours, hungry. Mikael understood when the woman lifted the trapdoor on the floor and started cooking. He wondered how many dinners there could be in a day in this world. Considering how slowly time passed, there should be quite a few meals. By now, they were up to three or four, but they had also been away from the house for almost eight or ten hours.

After the meal, the man took Mikael's hand and indicated that he should follow him to the inner room. Pernilla stood up to go with them, but the man held up his hand in a stop gesture. Mikael became worried at first, but when the man smiled and gestured for him to follow, he agreed. Inside the room, the man walked to one corner and lifted a trapdoor on the floor.

From the hole, he pulled up something wrapped in cloth. He held the small package in his hand and revealed its contents. It was a shiny revolver and a package of cartridges. He pointed at the revolver, grimaced, and bared his teeth. Mikael understood at once what he meant and felt proud of the man's trust in him.

The man showed that he trusted the boy by revealing the revolver's hiding place and that Mikael would help him protect his woman if a threat appeared when he was not in the house.

The day went on, and Mikael and Pernilla tried to pass the time with various activities: they practiced their language, learned to play a game the woman had shown them, explored every corner of the house – which didn't take long considering how small it was –, spent some time outside helping with the horse, and looked through the outbuildings to see if there was anything fun to do. They found a lot of planks and decided to try to build something.

"A chair," said Mikael, but Pernilla thought he was aiming too low. "Why not a sofa? With so much material here, I think we should go big." They worked for a long time. There was sawing and nailing, and eventually, it was finished. The man had checked on them from time to time but mostly just shook his head at their creation. It was a strange sofa.

Normally, you sit next to each other on a sofa, but not on this one. On this sofa, you sit in a row, one after the other. And with the chains attached to the ends, it could even be hung up in a tree.

The rest of the time, they continued trying to figure out a way to get back home. After all, that was their main goal. They wondered why the stone had managed to make it through and concluded it must have been the speed with which it came. And the weight, maybe. They weren't exactly Einsteins, but they had a bit of sense.

The day went on, and when the sun finally set over the horizon, and they lay there on the kitchen floor, which the woman had prepared for them, they thought of their families and how much they longed to go home. They lay in silence, and when Mikael's eyes started to cross, he turned onto his back with his back to Pernilla.

With tears still in his eyes, Mikael fell asleep. Pernilla turned toward him and placed her arm across his body. Then, they slept peacefully for a long time. Until hell broke loose. Mikael woke up as the woman shook him and called something in her language.

Mikael understood it was serious and sat up. Pernilla jumped up, screaming in panic. She had been woken from a nightmare, where the horrible creature had tried to eat her alive!

The woman continued pulling on Mikael, and he saw that the trapdoor on the floor was open. Now, he also heard the sound from outside, a gurgling roar, and he knew exactly where it came from.

Pernilla threw herself after Mikael and realized something terrible was about to happen. She saw the man go toward the door to bar it with the extra planks stacked nearby.

The moment the man lifted the first plank, the door came crashing in with such force that the man was pushed into the opposite wall and lay lifeless. The woman threw Mikael down through the trapdoor and grabbed Pernilla, doing the same with her. She then closed the trapdoor and just managed to cover it with the large, thick rug to hide its existence before the creature entered the house. Mikael and Pernilla lay completely silent in the food cellar.

Above, they heard the creature's continued roars and rampage. They heard the woman's screams as she was thrown into the fireplace to be silenced completely. There was no sound from the man, who hadn't woken up after the creature's entry, and they understood he must have fainted. The only sound he made was his last breath when the creature stabbed its fork straight into his stomach, but that sound never made it down to the food cellar.

The children were completely silent. They didn't even dare to move a bit, terrified that the trapdoor would be ripped open at any moment by the horrible creature. They heard it moving around up there, continuing to run amok, destroying everything in the house. Furniture being thrown around, glass shattering.

After that, there was complete silence for a short moment, except for the sound of a creaking floorboard right above them. They waited for the trapdoor to be torn open. Then they heard footsteps, something dragging, a door slamming into the wall.

A deep gurgling sound. They heard the horse's panicked whinnying as it was forced toward the cart. They heard two bodies thrown onto the back. Thud, thud! Then, the crunch of gravel as the cart's wheels began rolling away from the house.

Chapter 6

It wasn't easy to get through the last thick stretch of the forest. They had met a patrol in the form of large swirling thorn bushes almost right away after the small lake they had cooled off in, and after several hours of struggling, they finally appeared into a meadow.

Once out of the forest, they felt a lovely wind coming toward them. A pleasant, cooling breeze against their warm, sweaty bodies. It was hard to keep wearing the heavy clothes; they would have preferred to throw them off, but the wind still felt nice, and it did offer some relief.

Peter and Filip continued their journey along the edge of the forest. A little further ahead, they saw a high cliff that dropped straight down, and sure enough, there appeared to be a path winding ahead. They quickened their pace, and after a while, they were out on the gravel road. There, they spotted something resembling a house a little ways off. They saw a small path leading up to the house and the rocky cliff rising just behind it. There was also something resembling a chicken coop at the back.

"Should we go up? Maybe Mikael is there?" Peter asked.

"But isn't it too early? According to the description, it seems like it's still quite a way to go," Filip said, holding the map in front of him.

"Let me see," Peter said. "We might not be able to trust Mikael 100%. He might have messed up the proportions pretty badly. It's still a good idea to check; at least ask if anyone has seen him."

Filip agreed, and they headed towards the house, unaware of what had happened there just a day earlier. Completely unaware that the wellst, whom Mikael had shot right between the eyes and then left behind, thinking: 'he must be stone dead,' had come back to life.

The creature, whose brain mostly remained in its skull as a remnant of its earlier origin, was like a human appendix. A creature is more like a reptile, acting according to reflexes from its spine. A creature, now more terrifying than ever, more horrific than anyone could imagine. Chillingly awful in every way.

A true monster.

They slowed down the last stretch before reaching the house and examined it. It looked strange. More like a hut than a house. It appeared completely deserted; the door to the building was slightly ajar, and there were no signs of anyone living there. They decided to continue forward, with Peter leading.

At the hut, Peter pushed open the door and cautiously said, "Hello." When he received no response, he stepped inside the dark interior.

The smell hit him, and he had to cover his nose. He continued inward and waited a moment for his eyes to adjust to the darkness. To the right was a bed of grass, and a little further behind it, a large wooden box with the oats they had eaten earlier.

Straight ahead, a fireplace with a grate that he guessed functioned as a grill or oven, and to the left, a small table and a chair. Beside the fireplace stood a rack with a fire fork and a small ash shovel.

Peter moved toward the table, where the sunlight shone through a small crack in the wall and spotted a drawing lying there. He picked up the paper. He could tell it was of the same quality as the letter Mikael had given him, the same quality as the map he had left behind. He held it up to the little light coming through the crack and saw a drawing of a mountain glowing and crackling, with a small stick figure next to it. Next to the stick figure, it said: 'Mikael.'

"Look, Filip. Micke has been here."

Filip looked at the drawing and saw Mikael's name. "We're on his trail," he said, beaming.

At the same time, the door to the hut closed behind Peter and Filip.

Both quickly recoiled, shocked by the dreadful sight.

"Oh, damn," said Filip, turning around. "Let's go, we're leaving."

"Wait a second," said Peter, who had also turned around and was about to vomit. "I need to check again."

He had quickly closed his eyes when he saw the bodies inside. He hadn't seen much of them and wasn't sure if one of the bodies was Mikael. He had to check again.

Once he had gotten over the worst of the reaction, he cautiously peered in again. He could see the bodies of two adults. One was missing arms and legs, and the floorboards beneath them were stained with dried blood. Neither of them was Mikael. He was sure of it.

After a while, Peter finally calmed down. No trace of Mikael.

The drawing they had found inside the hut must have come here in another way. They pushed the door shut behind them, and before leaving, they glanced inside the hut once more to make sure that the monster they thought they had killed was still lying on the floor.

It was. And they were certain it was dead.

"Let me see the map," said Filip, extending his hand. Peter handed him the map.

"We came from here," Filip said, pointing to one of the lines Mikael had drawn. "That means we need to go back a bit and then turn right."

"Seems right. Come on, let's move," Peter said eagerly, heading toward his backpack.

"Do you have any more Pucko?"

"No, just water," Peter lied, having saved a bottle for Mikael.

They jumped onto the cart and got the horse moving. They traveled for several hours along the bone-dry gravel road. The heat was almost unbearable, but they kept going with only one goal in mind: to find Mikael.

A little further away in the sky, they saw a couple of large clouds approaching. They hoped for rain. A nice, refreshing rain. The clouds moved quickly toward them, and after a couple of hours, they could feel the first drops hitting their faces.

The sun was obscured, and it didn't take long before the temperature dropped to the normal summer levels, they were used to back home. It was wonderful when their warm clothes cooled down, and when their hats became soaked with rain, they could feel their strength beginning to return to their exhausted bodies.

"So nice," Filip shouted out loud. "Now, this is something."

"Yes, nice," Peter replied more modestly. Inside his mind, the worries had never stopped tormenting him. He couldn't let go of thoughts of Mikael. Would they find him? How long would they search before giving up? Preferably never, he told himself, but he also understood that they couldn't keep going forever. Sure, they hadn't been here that long yet, but he still wanted to be prepared for the worst. Mikael had been missing for ten years, and somewhere inside, he understood that he might never come back. And surviving for ten years in this crazy world!

"Try to speed up the old horse," Filip said energetically.

"You're crazy, take it easy. We don't know how much farther we have to go or what condition the horse is in. It might be old. And you do remember that it's Micke who drew the map!"

"Ha, ha," Filip chuckled. "Yes, I remember. And I also remember Timmerlunda treasure hunt day from ten years ago. Do you remember?"

Peter did. He also remembered how it all ended in chaos when one of the teams got lost that night and how Filip, not Mikael this time, turned out to be the guilty one and was eventually scolded by their parents.

***

It was a usual summer, really hot, and the parents of children in grade six were, as tradition dictated, going to organize a treasure hunt the weekend after school ended.

Under normal circumstances, during normal summers when it wasn't terribly hot, the treasure would be placed deep in the forest. Almost a mile in. But now it was decided that a couple of kilometers would be enough.

All the children and parents, including the Overstuffed brothers and their significantly overweight parents, gathered at the beach on Saturday morning and received their own maps. The teams could be formed however they liked: as a family, a group of friends, or anything in between. Just as long as no one went alone, that was taboo!

Of course, Peter, Filip, and Mikael were going to be a team. And they were going to win grandly; that was their plan. But when it was all over, it turned out they came dead last. What started out so well ended in complete disaster.

When the gong sounded, everyone ran in the same direction at first. But after about a kilometer, most people choose their own directions based on their own interpretations of the map. Two of the teams that chose the same direction were The Three Majestic and the Overstuffed family.

Peter, who was absolutely certain they had chosen the right path, told Mikael and Filip that they needed to try to mislead the Overstuffed somehow. That's when Filip came up with the perhaps not-so-brilliant idea of trying to steal their map.

When the Overstuffed family slowed down after a couple of kilometers, Filip saw his chance. The family sat down and took out sandwiches and drinks. Filip hesitated for a moment but finally went up and asked for something to eat.

When their mother broke off a piece of her sandwich to give to Filip, he seized the opportunity to sneak away their map. Filip quickly shoved the sandwich into his mouth and thanked them profusely.

After that, he turned on his heels and set off with Mikael and Peter along the route on the map.

Left behind, the Overstuffed family was without a map and had no idea how to continue. Neither toward the treasure nor back to Timmerlunda. For an entire day, they wandered around the Timmerlunda forest before finally managing to get home. Completely starving.

When the boys' parents later found out that it was their kids who were responsible for the Overstuffed family getting lost in the forest, they made sure to give them a proper lesson. The team was relegated to last place in the competition, and Filip received a good scolding, even from his dad, who had tried to hide a little grin on his face when he cursed those unflattering words at his beloved son.

"Stop for a moment," said Filip as they approached a side road.

Peter pulled on the reins, and the horse stopped.

"I'm thinking we should turn off here," he said, pulling out the map.

The side road was a bit smaller than the one they had been traveling on, and after checking Mikael's map, they concluded that it should be correct. They continued down the smaller road.

After about an hour, they saw a small house with an outbuilding. They were cautious and made sure it was the right house and not one of those where a monster might live. They were fairly sure there were more of that kind. Why wouldn't there be?

After sneaking around the house and trying to peek through the small window openings, they concluded that the house was empty. The door was ajar, and they went inside.

It was messy inside; tables and chairs were scattered about, and in one corner of the floor, there were blankets and pillows. Peter went over and lifted up one of the pillows. He first carefully smelled it, and when he thought he recognized the scent of Mikael, he pressed it harder against his face.

"We've got it right. Mikael lives here. Or at least used to live here."

"I know," said Filip. "I can tell by Micke's spelling."

Peter turned around and saw Filip reading a piece of paper that was taped to the wall. He hurried over to read it.

WE WERE SURPRISED BY THE MONSTER AND DIDN'T DARE STAY. PROMISE TO WATCH OUT FOR THE MONSTER.
WE DON'T KNOW WHERE WE SHOULD GO, BUT WE MUST GO ON. MICKE

"We," said Peter. "Which 'we'?"

"Probably, he lived here with someone else. Maybe a family who took care of him. So, he hasn't been alone all these years," Filip replied, tearing the paper from the wall.

It seemed completely natural for Filip and Peter to assume that Mikael must have been in this world for so many years. After all, it had been ten years since Mikael disappeared. Had they known that Mikael and Pernilla had left the house early that morning, their reasoning would have been completely different.

They started to explore the rest of the house for signs of Mikael. They first entered the inner room, but there was only a bed and a few other pieces of furniture.

Peter noticed the hatch in the floor when they came back into the first room and lifted it. He went down and saw the food that was stored there. It wasn't much, but enough so they could get something other than the roots they had tried from the fields. And the food they had brought in their backpacks was nearly gone.

"Check this out," he heard from above.

He brought some of the food up with him and placed it on the table. Filip was sitting on a chair, holding a bunch of drawings he had picked up from the floor.

"It looks like Micke drew these," he said, holding them up for Peter.

"But what seems strange is that it looks like he was at most twelve, thirteen years old when he drew them. Maybe it was a long time ago he lived here."

"Really," Peter said after looking through the drawings. "I agree, but it can't have been that long ago. Look at the vegetables I brought up from the basement. They look pretty fresh."

"Strange," Filip said after glancing at the vegetables. "But is there any point in staying to see if he comes back? I still think it must have been quite a while since he was here."

"We'll stay, fix some food, and figure something out. But it won't be easy to figure out where he might be. The only thing we can do, as I see it, is to continue down the larger road. We came from the other direction, and I don't think they could have gone that way. Considering the monster, we met," Peter concluded.

"Okay, let's go with that," replied Filip, and started looking through the pile of vegetables. He didn't recognize any of them, but they resembled potatoes, carrots, and some other vegetables he was familiar with from home.

They managed to get the stove going and made a soup, guessing that adding some of what looked like spices would work, which turned out to be a good decision. It tasted great, and they were properly full when everything had been eaten.

After the meal, they took the opportunity to fill their water bottles from the barrel they had discovered while making the soup. The water tasted surprisingly good, and once again, Peter wondered when Mikael could have been here last: 'Maybe it was fairly recent after all.'

They felt a bit tired after the meal and lay down on the floor by the blankets to rest. They propped up the pillows, arranged the blankets underneath them, and made themselves comfortable. They had agreed on resting for no more than an hour, after which they would set off again to continue their search for Mikael.

Chapter 7

It took a long time before they dared to leave the food cellar. They were terrified that the creature would still be above, sitting still at the table and discovering them when they opened the hatch. They didn't know how long they had been waiting, but it felt like several hours.

Silent and with their arms around each other, they stayed in the cellar. They had waited until the violent turmoil had subsided, then heard what they thought was the sound of a horse-drawn cart disappearing from the house.

Still, they couldn't be entirely sure. They also understood that the monster they had killed was not the only one here. There were more. They wondered if the one that had surprised them in the middle of the night looked the same as the one they had killed.

If they had seen it before the woman sent them down into the cellar, they would have noticed the hole in its forehead, realizing it was the same creature that Mikael had thought he killed earlier.

Mikael gathered his courage to lift the hatch. He slowly pushed it up but immediately discovered that the thick rug was in the way. He had to open it completely to see anything. When the hatch was fully open, they saw what they had hoped for: the house was empty. But they understood they had to leave quickly; the risk of the creature returning was too great.

They filled a basket with as much food as they could hold and climbed up from the cellar. They put on their outerwear to leave, but first, they placed a note for Peter in case he managed to find his way here and find the house empty. They didn't know where they would go, and Mikael was worried they wouldn't be found. But they absolutely couldn't stay here. The risk of the monster returning was too high.

As they were about to leave the house, Mikael suddenly remembered the revolver the man had shown him. He turned in the hallway and went back inside to get it.

On his way out again, he stopped and looked around the house. He wanted to remember how it looked. After all, it had been his home for a while, and he wasn't sure if he would ever see it again. He also thought of the woman and the man. They had been his temporary parents, and he already missed them. He was sad about what had happened and wished he had thought about the revolver earlier before the woman had pushed them into the cellar he had rushed into the inner room and grabbed the revolver then.

Maybe he could have saved them. But everything had happened so fast. And he had been surprised in his sleep.

Mikael and Pernilla left the house with no idea where they were going. Going back towards and past the monster, which could still be alive even though Mikael had shot it between the eyes, was not an option. They first had to leave the area and then try to find another way back to the mountain. They were determined to try to get back home as long as the mountain was open to them when they reached it.

They walked side by side on the gravel road leading to the first intersection. Then they turned right, hoping to find more options ahead.

They walked in silence, not saying anything to each other. Both felt down and couldn't really process what had happened to them. Pernilla was the one who had taken it the hardest. In her head, the events from the house replayed over and over again: the sound of the creature, the woman's screams, and the noise from their bodies as they were thrown onto the cart. She wished it was just a nightmare, that she would wake up and realize it had all been a dream.

She had been here for over a day now, but in her sense of time, it felt like over a week. And in the Timmerlunda world, more than ten years have passed. But, of course, she had no idea.

Mikael thought about his brother and wondered if he would ever manage to get here. Maybe he had already tried. Standing and waiting by the mountain even though nothing had happened. No shimmering light. No opening appeared, and no pulling force that had drawn him in, wanting to pull him away, sending him far, far away from home to the world his twin brother now found himself in.

His brother had succeeded. And he had Filip with him. The two of them were probably sitting, a little lost, by the mountain right now, wondering where they had ended up. Something Mikael, of course, had no idea about.

When Mikael and Pernilla reached the next intersection, they chose to turn left, trying to get around the entire area where they had spent their time in this strange world. For hours, they continued along the road and saw the giant sun slowly rise in the sky.

The heat from the sun grew stronger, but they could also hopefully see a solid cloud cover moving toward them from the opposite side of the sun. They hoped it would hold together and move toward the sunny side, eventually covering it completely. If they were to continue their journey on foot, they would need shade and, ideally, some cooling rain as well.

They got shade in the form of tall trees. They had now entered a dense forest with very tall trees, and the road grew narrower.

Pernilla noticed it first, a rumbling, deep sound that was barely audible. She felt it first in her body, in her lungs, and thought something was wrong with her. But after a while, she realized it came from somewhere else, far away.

When she stopped and asked Mikael if he heard any strange noise, he paused and listened. Now, he could hear it, too. It sounded like a continuous thunder sound that neither decreased in frequency nor strength but just kept grinding on. Not like a fighter plane flying overhead, dragging the sound with it in its direction. No, this sound didn't fade; it just kept grinding.

He thought he saw something moving out of the corner of his eye and looked into the forest. He didn't initially understand what it was, but when he concentrated, he saw how the ground was moving. It was as if the topsoil was slightly above the ground, and he assumed it was due to the vibrations. And now, he felt it in his legs too.

Curious, he tried to locate where the sound was coming from. He slowly turned his head from one side to the other, and when he stopped, he told Pernilla that they should continue along the road toward the field they could now see a little further ahead and then cut across it in the direction of the sound.

Pernilla was on board, and they continued forward at a faster pace, almost jogging until they reached the field. There, they turned in the direction of the sound.

About an hour later, they reached the edge of a ridge and could look down toward the source of the sound. They stood for a long time, stunned, contemplating the strange scene playing out below the slope. They saw something they had never seen before.

A barren surface stretching as far as the eye could see. A faint light mist of stone dust hovered over the ground below. The mountain was in daylight, and periodically, there were enormous holes. Closest, near the edge of the ridge below, a spectacle unfolded that left Mikael and Pernilla dumbfounded.

Something resembling a massive wooden wheel, lying down with a kind of drill in the center. The drill was about ten meters thick, and there was a mechanism that allowed it to be lowered into the center, ensuring that the spokes of the wheel always stayed at ground level. The wheel was approximately one hundred meters in diameter, and at each spoke, there were about fifty people pushing it in front of them, like rats in a hamster wheel. A drilling machine powered by humans. Or rather, wellsts.

"My God!" said Pernilla, completely taken aback by what she saw below.

"What are they drilling for, do you think?"

"No idea," replied Mikael. "But now we at least know where the sound is coming from."

The friction of the drill slowly cutting into the bedrock propagated through the surroundings, traveling far, far away. First inaudible, and only noticeable through vibrations in the ground that transferred into the body, up into the lungs. After that, the long, dark, deep rumble that felt as if it first sealed off the ears, an undefined, energy-filled background noise.

"Whatever they're drilling for, they seem to have been at it for a while, given all the holes," said Pernilla, pointing her hand toward the horizon.

Fascinated by what he saw, Mikael said, "It's those monsters. Do you see them? They must be thousands! Now we know there are more of them, at least."

When they looked more closely, they saw that the wellsts were chained, and people were urging them on with whips. They had made them their slaves. And upon the spokes, people walked around carrying vessels with water that they poured into recesses in the spokes.

The wellsts drank from them like livestock in a barn. Neither Mikael nor Pernilla could figure out what they were drilling for. They grew more and more curious and decided to find out.

A little further away was a large metal building, and via a rail, wagons were being brought in from one side. The rail was drawn from one of the previously drilled holes, where the drilling dust was shoveled into the wagons.

The wagons were pulled by the slaves to the building. A tall chimney spewed out a thick cloud of black smoke. They found a place where they hid the food and the revolver, then followed the ridge down diagonally toward the large metal building. They tried to blend into the surroundings as best they could.

They moved slowly to minimize the risk of being detected. They absolutely didn't want to be noticed. The people down there didn't seem particularly friendly.

When they got down from the slope, they followed one wall of the building and started looking for a hole or crack in the wall through which they could see inside. At one spot, the metal didn't reach all the way to the ground, and Mikael lay down to look inside. From what he could see, it looked like some sort of factory. On one side, there was a large vessel glowing, and further into the factory, there were huge rollers being pulled around by more wellsts. It smelled awful. Probably toxic, Mikael guessed.

Pernilla took a look, too, then they continued along the long wall until they reached the end. On the backside, gray metal plates were being packed into boxes, and only then did they realize that lead plates were being made there, probably for houses and clothing.

"I feel a little sorry for the monsters," said Pernilla. "No wonder they're so hostile toward humans when they're treated like this."

"Or maybe the monsters are just monsters, and in that case, I don't mind," Mikael replied.

"Remember, one of them might have killed the man and the woman. If it had discovered us, we'd probably be dead too. And the one that held you captive! You'd probably be eaten by now if we hadn't managed to rescue you. I think they're just naturally evil," Mikael concluded.

They were just about to turn around to leave when someone grabbed them by the neck.

The supervisor in the lead factory saw the two disappear behind the building. He told one of the workers to keep an eye on production and sneaked after them to find out what was going on.

Sometimes, metal plates were stolen, and now he thought he might be on the trail of the thieves. Lead plates were a hot commodity among the public, and selling plates 'on the side' could generate a lot of sought-after barter goods.

The supervisor was an unusually large person with a slightly peculiar appearance. Some claimed, behind his back, that he was a cross between a human and a wellst. His teeth were crooked but lacked razor-sharp edges. One of his eyes was positioned lower than the other, and he had more hair on his body than was normal. But really, he was just somewhat deformed. Both of his parents belonged to the humans of this world.

He reached the corner of the back and peeked out. He saw them looking in through the small hole in the wall that had yet to be fixed. He made a note to make sure it got done as soon as there was time. We've got plenty of metal, he thought as he stood there watching the two get up again.

As they continued forward, he followed and just managed to catch up with them at the far corner of the building.

"Now you bastards, I've got you," he thought as he grabbed them firmly by the neck.

"I've got you now, you damn thieves!" he shouted at them.

Mikael felt the pain in his neck and heard the large man roar, something Mikael naturally didn't understand. He looked at Pernilla and saw that she was nearly fainting from the man's strong grip.

"Let go!" he yelled in panic. "You're choking us!"

The man seemed momentarily taken aback when he saw what he had caught. Two deformed people, and it also seemed like they were children. He recoiled, and Mikael first thought the man was scared by his shout. But when the man recovered from the shock, he grabbed them by the neck again and shoved them in front of him out onto the courtyard. He shouted to one of the men nearby and told him to help.

"What the hell have you caught?" the man exclaimed, laughing. "Are these your kids?" he added but regretted it when the supervisor let go of one of the children to slap him hard across the face.

"Now that was funny, you little brat. Help me get them into the barracks, and we'll figure out what to do with them later. These little pigs were snooping behind the corner, probably to steal some metal."

The man touched his cheek and carefully avoided making eye contact with the foreman. He grabbed Pernilla and followed the supervisor and Mikael to the barracks. They were thrown to the floor, and the door was locked behind them.

"Dammit," Mikael shouted into the darkness, then heard Pernilla start crying.

"I want to go home. I miss Mom," sobbed Pernilla, sitting with her arms wrapped around her legs, pressed against her body.

"Me too," Mikael said resignedly, now thoroughly tired of all the crap they had been through. "I'm tired of this world now. I just want to go home. Back to Peter and Fille. And Mom."

In fact, he even missed the brothers, stuffed to the brim; seeing them now would make him incredibly happy. And the Swedish teacher at school. Even though she constantly complained about Mikael's spelling and that they didn't always get along, he'd run and jump into her arms if he saw her right now.

"What do you think will happen now?" asked Pernilla, who had now started to make out Mikael's shape in the dark.

"I don't know. If we could just talk to the people here, maybe we could get them to understand. Maybe they think we're thieves."

"Probably."

Time dragged on, and it felt like they had been sitting in the barracks for an eternity when the man finally came back and opened the door. The noise and vibrations from the drill had settled into their minds, and they just wanted to get out of there.

Anywhere, just away.

When the door opened wide, the barracks was filled with fresh air, but the freshness was at once replaced by the man's sweaty body odor.

I wonder if I smell that bad too, Mikael thought as he felt the stench from the man.

I need a shower, thought Pernilla.

The man tied the children's hands with a rope and pushed them out of the barracks. Once their eyes had adjusted to the bright light, they saw a strange vehicle of some sort parked outside in the gravel yard. Mikael thought it looked like something he had seen in a schoolbook, but not exactly the same.

The vehicle had four wheels, and so far, everything seemed normal. But the huge barrel that should have been in the front of the vehicle, according to the schoolbook, was now in the back, with pipes running in and out. And next to it, another barrel was emitting smoke.

The steering mechanism was at the front, and a flatbed followed. The man hoisted Mikael and Pernilla onto the flatbed with a lot of noise. Mikael felt the rough floor scrape his face on one side, and Pernilla screamed in pain as she bounced into the rear gate. The man sat down and pulled on a couple of levers, and the vehicle began to move.

Two larger men jumped up and sat beside the man, and when the vehicle gained speed, they had to hold tightly to the sides to avoid falling off. The vehicle lacked shock absorbers and jerked from side to side. The wheels, made of metal and wood, struggled to gain traction in the soft gravel.

Mikael and Pernilla tried to sit as comfortably as possible, but every time they found a comfortable position, the vehicle jolted, and they had to start over.

In the chaos, a memory stirred inside Mikael's mind. A memory from the summer break, when Mikael, Peter, and

Filip came across a steamroller, standing all alone, just waiting to be test-driven. And how they managed to turn it into a self-driving weapon.

***

They had walked along the main street in Timmerlunda, heading away from the center. They turned right, down toward the new parking lot that was being prepared outside the local ICA store. And at the far end, next to piles of sand and gravel, it had stood. The steamroller.

It was a late evening, and twilight was approaching. The crickets were playing their violins, and the warm day was turning into a cooler, more humid evening. Peter had spotted it first.

"Look! A steamroller," he said, pointing at it.

"Wow," said Mikael with his mouth open and eyes wide. Filip looked around and noted that they were completely alone at the location. No one was nearby.

"Come on, let's check it out," he said, heading toward the corner of the intended parking lot where the steamroller stood. The twins followed him.

When they arrived, the boys jumped onto the steamroller and started pulling at the controls and pressing the pedals. It was an old-fashioned open model without a roof. Not very big.

"How do you think you start it?" Mikael asked, eager for some action.

"Come on, we're not driving it," said Filip, laughing.

Mikael started looking for a key of some sort. He first checked under it, inspected every nook and cranny, then continued upwards. When he slid his hand between the seat cushion and the spring beneath, he felt something. And sure enough, it was a key.

"The key!" he shouted, holding it up in front of the others.

"Quiet," said Peter, glaring at Mikael. "Do you want the whole village to hear you?"

"Let me see," said Filip, extending his hand.

Mikael handed Filip the key, who quickly scanned the dashboard, searching for the ignition lock.

"There," Mikael shouted when he spotted a hole where the key seemed to fit.

"Quiet," said Peter and Filip, whispering in unison.

"Oops, sorry," Mikael said. "I got carried away a bit."

"Yeah. Think a little," said Peter, looking back.

Mikael felt a bit embarrassed and took a step back. He often got too eager and had trouble holding back. It was just his way. But it was also what defined Mikael. Impulsive and not always very thoughtful. But it was also that quality that made him who he was. Creative and fun, for the most part.

Filip inserted the key into the ignition and turned it. With a jump, the steam roller started moving and began moving forward relentlessly, heading toward the adjoining lawn that bordered the river running through the village.

Earlier, when the boys had been tugging at the controls, they had accidentally put the gearstick in the 'forward' position. Now, with Peter and Filip on top and Mikael trailing behind, they frantically tried to make it stop.

Peter pulled at all the controls he could reach while Filip tried to turn the ignition key back to the stop position. The key seemed stuck, in some strange position, and when Filip finally managed to turn the key, it broke in half, and the steamroller continued its course over the lawn. And it was only about ten meters left to the river.

With only a meter to go, Peter and Filip jumped off. The steam roller kept going, and the three boys stood still a bit behind, watching as it slowly drove over the edge and plunged into the water with a loud splash.

The river was deep at that spot, and by the time the boys reached the water, the steamroller was gone. It bubbled in the water for a brief moment, but then everything went silent and calm.

Filip looked around for the second time that evening and could once again confirm that they were completely alone on the spot.

For Mikael, this had happened just a few weeks ago, and the memory of the event was still fresh. But in Timmerlunda, it had now been almost fifteen years. His classmates from sixth grade were adults, and many of them had even become parents.

The new school building that housed the middle school students turned out to be a major shoddy construction and had been badly attacked by mold. It was torn down in 1984, and no replacement building was ever constructed.

Instead, students were bussed to the larger town of Rågmanstorp.

And the steamroller? Well, no one really knows what happened to it.

A lot had happened since Mikael stepped into the twin world. If he ever made it back, it would be with great surprise what had happened to little Timmerlunda since he disappeared that Saturday night in 1977.

Mikael was snapped out of his daydream when the vehicle suddenly shook violently. They had stopped. He stood up to get a better view of the surroundings. Pernilla was deeply asleep, curled up in one of the flatbed corners, unaware of what was going on. Mikael hoped she was dreaming of something beautiful from home.

Mikael saw a high wall winding off, and at one end, there was a gate guarded by armed men. From what he could gather, he guessed that there might be a settlement on the other side, but when he saw smoke rising from tall chimneys, he suspected it might also be yet another industrial area.

The supervisor yanked a lever, and the vehicle started moving forward toward the gate. After they were let in and continued down a main road lined with low buildings, Mikael realized it was a community where people lived. The houses were simply built with metal-covered walls and roofs, and everything was covered with a thin layer of road dust. A bit like the houses back home in Timmerlunda during the driest summers.

The dust swirled around as they traveled down the street. People walked along the road, and here and there, one could make out small, simple shops and food stalls.

The food stands were small holes in the wall, with food served through a window. The scent of food filled the air, and Mikael felt his mouth begin to water. They hadn't had a proper meal since their foster parents were taken away so dramatically. Mikael wondered if they were still alive.

The people lining the street wore heavy, clumsy, lead-covered clothing, but they seemed to be doing fine. At least they looked happy.

Maybe they have it good here, Mikael thought, feeling the beginnings of a smile. A smile that wouldn't last too long.

The journey continued through the village, and after a few turns, the vehicle stopped in front of a building that was slightly taller than the other structures. Pernilla had now woken up and wondered where on earth they had ended up. Mikael had no good answer to that question, so she had to settle for an educated guess.

The man yelled at them, and they understood that he wanted them to jump down from the flatbed. Mikael and Pernilla scrambled over the edge and tried to hold back as much as they could with their tied hands to avoid injuring themselves from the fall. But still, they hit the gravel and ended up in a heap of arms and legs.

"Watch out!" Mikael yelled, trying to get Pernilla out from under him.

The man grabbed them both by the arms and dragged them into the building.

Chapter 8

They woke up inside the house to the sunlight that had made its way through one of the kitchen windows. The rays hit Peter right in the eyes as they lay in the corner of the room.

"Fille, how long have we really been asleep?" exclaimed Peter, nudging Filip. Filip slowly turned over and stretched his arms.

"Not long, I guess. Feels like I just fell asleep," he replied groggily, pulling his arms back and rubbing his crusted eyes.

"I had a dream," he continued in a tired voice.

"Right after I fell asleep, I dreamed I opened a Licorice bar. Just when I got the paper off, you woke me. Couldn't you have waited a bit longer so I could finish eating it?"

"Crazy," Peter replied as he stood up.

"We need to get going," he added, walking over to the window. He looked outside and saw that the sun had moved quite a bit. He suspected they'd been asleep for a long time, and now panic started creeping in. He wanted to continue searching for his twin brother, whom he hadn't seen in ten years.

"Come on, Fille," he said, stuffing the vegetables they had found into a wooden box. Filip crawled up, and they grabbed their backpacks and left the house.

The large bale of hay they'd given the horse earlier was now nearly eaten. The trough, which had been filled with water when they arrived, was also almost empty.

Peter grabbed the reins and turned the horse and cart around, then they jumped on and headed back toward the larger gravel road.

"No point in going back the way we came from. Take a right," suggested Filip, who was finally starting to wake up. Peter agreed and pulled on the reins so the horse turned right.

The horse trotted down the road, and the sun shone directly into their eyes. The sky was completely cloudless, and they understood they'd have a warm journey ahead. How far they had to travel, they didn't know. Nor did they know if they were heading in the right direction, but they assumed they had chosen correctly, at least, they hoped so. They leaned back, sitting in silence without saying a word, but their minds were busy with activity.

Filip had avoided asking Peter how he'd been since things went wrong between them after Peter had messed up and distanced himself as a friend. He had even slapped him! Filip knew Peter had struggled with alcohol, but he didn't know how serious it had gotten.

A few times, Peter had reached out to Filip, but each time, it had been when he was drunk. With his father still fresh in his mind, Filip didn't want to have anything to do with Peter unless he quit drinking. He didn't want to experience that betrayal again, losing someone he loved. Now, he felt it was time to take the bull by the horns and clear up the questions.

Inside Peter's mind, a different battle was raging, one between hope and despair. The hope of finding Mikael and the despair of not being able to find him. A text popped up somewhere in his memory. Strong words had been etched into him from a history lesson he barely remembered, but the words the teacher had read were still there.

A quote from Dante when he descends into hell and reads the text above the gate: "Abandon all hope, ye who enters here." If this is hell, should I give up hope then? Peter thought. He refused. He would never give up hope of finding his brother. If he had made it this far, he would find him. He was on the trail; he knew it. And he had also read the texts Mikael had left behind. He was close now, and he wouldn't give up. That was out of the question.

Filip gathered his courage and asked, "Don't you ever crave alcohol?" Peter was taken aback. What does he mean? But at once, he reconciled with reality. Of course, he was wondering.

Although he had been a real jerk all these years, if Filip asked, he had reason to. Peter knew that. He thought for a moment about how to respond. Honestly, he didn't crave beer or liquor right now, but he also knew it was because his thoughts were consumed with Mikael at the moment. But now that Filip had mentioned it, sure, a beer would go down well.

"No, not right now, at least," he lied.

"But thanks for caring."

"Of course, I care. You know how things went with Dad."

"Yeah, but..." he began, ready to make an excuse but caught himself mid-lie. Filip is a true friend. He didn't hesitate for a second to help find Mikael. Don't lie! Admit it! The voices inside him urged him to answer honestly, and he gave in. Immediately!

"You're right, Filip. I know I have a problem. But if we find Micke, everything will change. I'm sure of it. Completely sure!"

"From now on, I'll support you. Whether we find Micke or not. But of course, we will find him. No doubt about it! I feel like we're close now!"

"I hope you're right. I don't know how much longer I can stand it now that we're so close. We have to find him."

"You can relax, we'll find him," Filip said, pulling Peter closer. At the same time, they began to feel vibrations traveling up through the wooden wheels, up to the seat of the cart. Peter had a flashback to that summer—the big one when they stole their brothers' super-tuned Puch Dakota.

***

Mikael and Peter had been heading toward the lake, passing the gravel pit, when they saw the brothers, who were stuffed with food, riding around on their older brother's moped. Envious, they watched as the overstuffed brothers raced around in the gravel. Up one of the gravel piles and down the other side. Sliding and steering in the soft sand. A bit like motocross. The moped was heavily tuned. The carburetor had been changed, and the plug had been pulled.

The top was smoothed against their garage floor, and a Snucko exhaust system had been installed instead of the boring, quiet one that came stock. And as the icing on the cake, there was a Cuppini rudder installed to make all other mopeds look boring in comparison. The brothers had taken the moped when their older brother went away with friends to the coast to swim, and now, as the twins watched, they were pushing it to its limits.

The moped came speeding over one of the obstacles. One brother was giving the other a ride, and when the moped went up on its back wheel and they both flew off, the twins screamed with joy. The moped made a turn, gently slid into the sand, and died. It went completely silent.

After a while, they went over to check if the brothers were still alive. Both were motionless and completely knocked out but still breathing. They took long, deep breaths, and the twins concluded that the brothers had passed out from the tough crash. They quickly saw their chance. They set the moped upright and started running with it between them.

When they reached a downhill slope, Peter jumped on and shifted the gears. When it started, he quickly pulled the clutch and hit the brakes. Mikael caught up and jumped on the back. They disappeared in the direction of the lake, where Filip was waiting. They had a great day, taking turns riding the moped until the fuel ran out and finally rolling it back to the gravel pit. The overstuffed brothers had come to and were gone from the place.

They leaned the moped against a tree and quickly left the area. Their prank was never discovered, and the brothers, stuffed with food, took the entire blame.

The gravel crunched against the wooden wheels, and the vibrations increased in intensity. Peter looked up at the trees and could swear they were swaying in unison with the long, slow vibrations from the ground. Down by the root system, he saw how the earth was lifted up, shifted, and exposed the roots beneath. Peter felt a little worried that a tree might fall, but they continued along the road anyway.

The vibrations became stronger and more intense the farther they went, and after a while, they saw a tree lying across the road a short distance ahead.

"Well, it looks like the road ends here," said Filip, standing up to get a better view. "No chance we can get that giant tree off the road."

The tree was enormous. Clearly over fifty meters long and maybe one and a half meters in diameter. It would take a powerful tractor to move it off the road, or it would need to be sawed into small pieces to be rolled away.

"We have no choice. We'll have to turn back," said Peter, who had just stepped off the cart to lead the horse around when he heard a crash behind him. He turned around and saw another equally large tree coming down toward them.

Peter shouted to Filip to watch out while releasing the reins from the horse and started running away from it. Filip wasn't as quick and barely managed to jump off the cart before the tree came down right on top of him. Debris flew from both the tree and the gravel road, and the horse and cart were enveloped in a cloud of dust.

When the sound from the fall died down and the vibrations from the ground were once again audible, Peter, who had managed to get to safety a bit off to the side, called out, "Filip!" but got no answer.

The dust from the road was still swirling in the air when Peter reached what remained of the cart. The horse stood motionless and silent beside it, and it was a miracle it hadn't panicked. Maybe it's deaf, Peter thought as he continued calling Filip's name.

When the dust cloud cleared, and he saw the remains of the cart, he prepared himself for the worst: that Filip had been crushed by the weight of the tree and that he had now left this world behind, even though he was in another realm.

"Damn, we should have turned back as soon as we saw the trees swaying," Peter thought as he started lifting the wreckage that used to be a cart. He pulled and tugged at the planks to move them aside, feeling the splinters from the worn boards attacking his hands. But he ignored them; his only goal in sight was getting Filip out. He hadn't given up hope yet.

When he cleared away one of the planks, he could make out Filip's body underneath. He reached in with his hand to check on him, to see if there was any life left, to check if he still had a pulse.

He managed to stretch his hand far enough to grab Filip's wrist and waited in anticipation for a sign of life.

He felt something.

There was still hope, and Peter began removing the planks more systematically. He was careful not to make the situation worse, not to yank off any plank that was stuck too hard and might cause a collapse like pick-up sticks.

He now saw that one of the wheels had become sideways and was wedged tight against one of the thick beams forming the cart's frame.

And underneath, shielded by the wheel, lay Filip, seemingly unharmed.

Peter sighed in relief and grabbed Filip's legs to pull him out. At first, it went well, but when Filip's shoulder got stuck in the narrow gap between the wheel and the beam, it came to a halt. Either he needed to apply more strength or somehow widen the opening. He at once saw that he couldn't move the wheel and decided to keep pulling.

He braced one leg against the tree trunk and yanked, and out came Filip, flying like a cork from a champagne bottle.

He dragged Filip into the forest and tried to rouse him.

Their life together flashed before Peter's eyes. From the first time they met outside Filip's house, the day Peter and Mikael moved to Timmerlunda. It was summer, and they were seven years old, with just a week left before starting school.

Filip, who was shorter than both Mikael and Peter at that time, beamed like the sun and was full of anticipation about who these two identical boys could be. He knew they had moved into the house at the end of the road, but that was all. Now, he wanted to get to know them.

They became fast friends right away, and ever since, they have been best friends until that day when Peter punched Filip. But if only Filip could wake up again, Peter would give back all the years they had been apart.

Make up for every little minute. From now on, they will be inseparable. And when Mikael was found, they would be the three of them again. Best friends for life. Just like they had promised each other when summer vacation began in 1977.

Peter began checking Filip's legs and arms. Nothing seemed broken, and he didn't see any other injuries except for a serious wound on one arm. He tore off a bit of string from his clothes and tied it just tightly enough above the wound. It wasn't bleeding much, but he still wanted to be on the safe side. Then he grabbed Filip and shook him while calling his name.

No response.

He shook him again, harder this time.

Still no response.

He hurried back to the cart to try to find the water they had brought with them, pulled and tore through the wreckage, and finally found a bottle. He took it back with him and, in passing, unscrewed the cap and prepared to pour some water on Filip.

"Good God. Please make Filip wake up," he thought as he let the water pour over Filip's face.

He saw the water wash over his face, trickling into his nose and mouth, filling his eye sockets and running down into his ears. At first, nothing happened, but after a few seconds, Filip coughed and took a deep breath.

Filip opened his eyes and sat up. "What happened?" he asked, stunned by the event, and immediately added, "Ow."

Peter smiled and threw himself over Filip.

"Ow, I said!" Filip screamed and pushed Peter away.

"Oh, sorry. I was just so happy you woke up," said Peter, pulling back. "Where does it hurt?"

"Here, on the side of my hip," answered Filip, holding his right side.

"It's a miracle you're still alive, you know. You ended up under the cart with the tree on top of you. The wheel is what saved you. Can you stand up, do you think?"

Filip tried but had to give up almost immediately. However, he managed to get to his knees and rocked from side to side to gauge how bad it was. Then he said, "Could be a crack. I don't think it's broken, though."

"We'll have to take it easy for a while. But first, we need to get out of the forest. That's priority one right now, before another tree falls. We'll try to get you on the horse; that's the only solution I can see."

"Whatever," said Filip, lying back down. His head was starting to spin, and he felt like he was about to faint.

"Drink some water, and I'll go to the cart and try to get our stuff."

He went back to the cart and returned after a while with the horse and backpacks. He also managed to get the vegetables from the wreckage, the ones they had brought from home. Some had been squashed under the cart, but most of them were still salvageable.

With great effort and many "Oh" from Filip, Peter finally got him onto the horse. He was grateful it was such a small horse. Had it been a normal-sized one, he probably wouldn't have been able to get him up.

They wound their way along the road, making detours around several fallen trees. Eventually, they were out of the forest and camped by a lonely tree on a field that provided some shade. Peter had noticed that someone or some people had recently crossed the field.

The grass was flattened like a trail, leading across the field toward the rise in the distance. They would follow it later when Filip felt better, which would take some time. They would spend most of the day under the tree until Filip was well enough to walk again. But after that, when they made it over the rise and saw the spectacle Mikael and Pernilla had already seen, they would be rewarded for their efforts.

Chapter 9

Mikael and Pernilla were approaching the end of the corridor and could now see the illuminated double door. The flames of the torches on the wall emitted a faint flickering light that gave the scene a frightening appearance. The walls lacked color, and cobwebs covered nearly every square inch of the surface, much like being in a barn that hadn't been cleaned in a hundred years. The floor felt more damp now than at the beginning of the corridor, and they understood they were deep underground.

The man pushed them against the wall and knocked three times on the door. He then slid a piece of paper under one of the doors, and after a few seconds, they heard a rustling sound from the other side. The door slowly creaked open.

The man grabbed them by the neck and led them through the door.

On the other side, there was full activity. They had entered a large cavern illuminated by hundreds of torches, and across the room, a path led up where a horse-drawn carriage was coming down. It had a large trailer behind it, resembling an animal transport, and was pulled by six horses. The floor was lined with men holding whips and rifles, and between them, they could see monsters crouching in a long row, seemingly terrified and nervous.

On the right side of the room, elevated by a set of stairs, they saw something both Mikael and Pernilla had encountered before: the glow and crackling sound from the rock wall where they had both been brought into this strange world. But this was a different portal. A portal to a completely different world.

A world full of monsters!

How had they managed to find this portal deep underground? If they had found it, could there be a chance they could find the portal to their own world? To Timmerlunda?

Mikael felt Pernilla's hand on his and how they tightened. He understood she was scared. He was, too.

The glow in the wall came well after well. Drugged and incapacitated, they had been gathered together by sent-out troops. For years, they had been brought from their world into this one to work as slaves in the giant lead fields that had grown up in the wake of the intense solar activity, to provide humans here with the only protection that helped against the electronic storms their planet was constantly bombarded with.

Mikael responded to Pernilla by squeezing her hand tightly. Then he felt the grip on their necks return. They were led forward to a barrack and shoved through a rear opening. The barrack was made of wood and stank of rot from the moisture in the rock foundation. An oil lamp hung at a slant from the ceiling, casting a dim light that barely helped. Mikael and Pernilla had to concentrate to even see what was happening inside.

The man holding their necks gave the paper he had received to another man and exchanged a few words with him.

After quickly scanning the paper, the man pondered for a moment and then said something neither Mikael nor Pernilla understood. The man with the neck grip laughed and smirked at them. Mikael did not see this as a good sign and feared the worst, whatever that might mean.

"Just as long as they don't send us to the monster world, I'll accept any punishment," he thought as they were both shoved out of the barrack.

The man led them to the horse-drawn carriage, which had now turned around. When they approached, he stopped and waited for the ongoing procedure. The monsters were being herded in like livestock. One by one, they were shoved into the transport carriage, and Mikael counted over twenty of them.

When the last monster was pushed in, the man continued toward the carriage's opening. Both Mikael and Pernilla understood what was about to happen and at once began to struggle. They screamed and flailed, terrified of what awaited them. But it was of no use.

When they were pushed into the carriage, they were hit by a horrendous stench, and Pernilla couldn't hold it back. A cascade of vomit came out of her, hitting the nearest monsters. They immediately recoiled as if afraid of what had come from her.

Mikael understood it was the smell of the vomit that made them back away, and soon, the others followed suit, pushing further into the carriage, away from Pernilla.

Mikael wrapped his arms around Pernilla and pulled her into a corner of the carriage. They sat there, far away from the others. To their advantage, it seemed they were left alone throughout the journey, all thanks to Pernilla's vomiting.

Mikael thought he needed to distract Pernilla; she was shaking and shivering in his arms, and he could tell she wasn't feeling well. He thought back to the events of the summer and stopped when he remembered a day when he had climbed the family's tall willow tree alone. He had climbed its climb-friendly branches and eventually reached the top. There, he found a position where he could lie still, eyes fixed on the sky.

Swallows zipped by in search of insects, and he had thought, "If I were to die and be born again, I would want to live as a swallow. Fly around like a little military plane."

"Pernilla," he whispered softly. When she muttered a faint "Yes," he asked, "If you were to die and be born again, what animal would you want to be?"

Pernilla thought for a moment and then replied, "Definitely not a clam at the bottom of the sea," before laughing lightly. "No. I'd probably want to be born as a bird. Maybe a swallow."

"What!" Mikael responded, surprised. "Is that true?"

"Yeah. What about it?"

"Same as me. I'd also want to be born as a swallow," he replied excitedly.

He tightened his grip on her, smiled, and thought: We belong together, you and me.

After they had gotten used to the stench, they managed to sleep for a while. There were small openings at the top of each long side where light and air could get in, making the journey slightly less uncomfortable. But it was still a relief when they finally arrived at their destination when the doors opened, and they were let out.

"Well, here we are again," Mikael said, shaking his head when he saw they were back at the lead fields. "So unbelievably pointless. First, a ridiculously long journey to the village, and then back the same way."

Pernilla took Mikael's hands and leaned against him. She couldn't make a sound. She felt disoriented from the journey and still felt ill. She was scared of what would happen to them now that they were back at the lead field. Would they have to work as slaves with the monsters? Or was something else unpleasant going on? Whatever punishment they received, she didn't expect it to be a pleasant experience.

They were pulled out from the back of the carriage, and immediately after, the monsters were released. Men with whips drove them forward toward the field, and after a few minutes, they were gone.

Mikael and Pernilla were taken into the large building, where their hands were freed. At first, Mikael thought this was a good sign, but when a man approached with a kind of belt that had metal rings on each side to be fastened around their waists, he realized: "Now it's time to work."

They walked through the building and came out on the other side. The man escorting them was large and fat and smelled as if he hadn't washed in weeks: a stench reminiscent of the monsters' smell.

Maybe he had become so accustomed to their scent that he had simply adopted it? Maybe he even liked it!

They continued toward the field, and Mikael was convinced they were going to be tied to a wheel alongside the monsters to push it until they couldn't go any further, exploited until they were too weak to contribute any more strength. But when they reached the wheel, they were instead lifted onto a platform of some kind attached to one of the spokes. From up on the spoke, they could see a thick rope running from the outermost point all the way to the hub.

A stretch of about fifty meters. And from the view up there, they now saw the spectacle up close. They could feel the atmosphere of the horrific situation the monsters were in. The smell from the sweaty monsters, the sound of the whips cracking in the air, constantly urging them to push harder. The thick fog from the dust swirled as the drill burrowed deeper and deeper into the lead-rich bedrock.

The man above waved for two others, who were standing a bit out on the spoke. Slowly, they moved toward the end, each carrying a large water jug. When they arrived, the rope was detached, and the jugs were handed over to Mikael and Pernilla.

"Goddamn, Pernilla. Now it's going to be a hell of a struggle," Mikael said, looking completely defeated.

"Don't swear," Pernilla said sulkily and added, "Look at it this way. At least we won't have to walk around pushing the wheel."

"I don't know if this is better, now that I think about it. If we had ended up down there, maybe we could have been forced to push. Now they'll be watching us more closely, and when I feel the weight of the jug, which is only half-full right now, I don't know."

"Don't swear!"

The man sent the two others down and then threaded the rope through Mikael and Pernilla's belts. He showed them where to fill the jugs with water and pointed to the depressions on the top of the spoke.

Both Mikael and Pernilla understood what was needed and began to fill the jugs at the barrel on the platform. Then they set off along the spoke to give the enslaved monsters some water.

Chapter 10

It felt like they had been on the grass field for several days. All the food they had brought from the house was gone, and their last few meals had only consisted of ears of grain. Peter had found the water a bit further away, and it had meant many trips back and forth. The horse also needed to be provided with water.

He was grateful for the shade from the tree, but the constant, persistent vibrations from the ground were something he would have gladly done without. It had been worse at the beginning. At that point, he thought he was going to lose his mind if it didn't stop soon, but now, after some time had passed, it was just annoying.

Filip was definitely on the mend and could now move almost freely. Mostly, they had been lying in the grass, talking about old memories, but Peter had periodically encouraged Filip to move in order to help the injury heal. He was afraid that if he stayed still for too long, it would do more harm than good. He believed that just the right amount of rest and movement in between would be the key to the quickest healing. And as it turned out, he was right.

Peter left Filip for a while and followed the path toward the crest to see where the sound and vibrations were coming from. But as he got closer, he saw that the path veered into a small grove of trees, so he followed that instead. After walking for a while, he saw a small bundle pressed under one of the trees, and when he opened it, a revolver and several cartridges fell out.

Mikael, he thought. He was convinced it was Mikael who had left it there. He felt it deeply within himself, just as only a twin could feel. An invisible bond that stretched through everything and connected the two individuals.

I wonder if Mikael feels me, he thought before hurrying back to Filip.

When the sun had passed its zenith and started sinking a bit in the sky, they decided to move on. They made sure the horse had food and water before setting off. Filip got to decide the pace, and at first, they moved slowly. But as he regained more movement in his body, the pace increased more and more. Eventually, it was Peter who had to tell Filip to slow down a little.

When they reached the crest and saw what was happening down below, they were completely stunned. It was the first time they had seen any form of civilization since they had arrived. It wasn't a pleasant sight, but still, they stood there for a long time, watching the spectacle. They wondered and discussed what was happening down there and finally agreed it was some kind of open-pit mining operation. But they didn't understand what they were digging for.

Just like Mikael and Pernilla had done earlier, they decided to try and get closer.

After walking for a while down the slope, they sat down. Now they had gotten so close that they could almost smell the monsters' foul, stale breath, see their sharp teeth sticking out from their jaws, and see the whips lashing through the air, urging them to push harder. They saw people walking around on the spokes of wheels, giving them water. Peter also saw two smaller children helping with the watering.

Barely older than we were that summer, Peter thought when he saw the two pouring water for one of the monsters.

For some reason, he couldn't take his eyes off them. Or rather, one of them. The boy. His posture. How he moved. His appearance. Almost exactly like Mikael from ten years ago.

"Filip! Do you see the boy down there? On the wheel, a little to the right."

"The one to the left?"

"I said to the right. You fool!"

"Yeah, yeah. What about him?"

"The little boy who's pouring water right now. Do you see him? Look at his appearance."

"But! It's Micke," Filip shouted, excited, and stood up.

"I know... or, at least, an exact copy. Because it can't be Micke; that one down there can't be older than Micke was when he disappeared," said Peter, realizing it must be that way.

But still not.

Somewhere deep inside him, there was something telling him it was Mikael. He saw him the way he looked the year he disappeared.

What if it really is Mikael? That something in this world made him stop growing? Surely that could be the case, right? Or not? So many strange things had already happened to them, he thought. Just the fact that they had made it here through a crackling, lit mountain wall. From one world to another. A parallel world.

"Filip, we have to go down. What if it is Mikael? That something in this world makes things slower than back home. Just think about how long the days are here!"

Filip thought. He wondered if it could be so. How much time had passed back home since they came over here? How long had Mikael been here? Maybe only a year, not ten? Or maybe five? He would get Mikael's answer to his question later. An answer he certainly hadn't expected.

"Okay. But how are we going to get down without being spotted?" Filip said, slinging on his backpack.

"I don't know. Got any good ideas?"

"We can take a chance. If we get spotted, maybe they'll think we belong to the staff?" Filip suggested, looking at Peter.

Peter thought for a moment and said, "Okay. That's probably our only chance. But we'll have to leave the backpacks here. I don't think they have ones like these."

They took off their backpacks and placed them behind a rock. But before they left, Peter took the revolver, checked it was fully loaded, and tucked it into his waistband under his lead vest.

"Okay. Try to blend in now," he said as they began their descent from the slope.

Filip held out his hand in front of Peter to stop him: "Maybe you want me to take that instead? I'm thinking I've got a bit more experience with weapons than you."

"You're right," Peter answered without hesitation, glad for Filip's suggestion. "You probably aim better than I do, too, if it comes to that."

"Yeah. But not as well as Mikael. You remember the carnival," Filip said, smiling at Peter.

Peter did and smiled back. He was glad that Filip was with him.

Chapter 11

The man at the end of the oak barked and shouted at Mikael and Pernilla to hurry up. The words, which neither of them understood, still carried a very clear message.

They hurried to give the monsters water, emptied their carafes, and then went back to refill them. It wasn't easy to move on top of the oak. For one, it was difficult to keep balance because the wheel kept tilting, almost stopping before suddenly picking up speed again. It was also hard to get the rope to run freely through the iron rings as they moved back and forth.

When they came out to refill the carafes for the fiftieth time, Mikael received a blow from the man that almost made him fall off the dock.

"What the hell are you doing?" Mikael shouted, holding his ear.

Pernilla bent down to check on Mikael.

The man shoved her aside and grabbed Mikael to give him another smack but was suddenly stopped by someone grabbing his arm.

"Leave him alone, you fool," Filip shouted, pressing the revolver straight to the man's face.

Mikael froze, not understanding what he had just heard. But then it dawned on him. Someone else from their world, he thought before he let his gaze seek the person who had come to their rescue. When he squinted up at the person, he saw not only one figure but two. And instantly recognized one of them.

Twins. There's something special about them. They recognize each other from miles away, sensing each other's presence even when they shouldn't. And that's how it was now. They were ten years apart, yet Mikael knew it was Peter standing there. How that was possible didn't matter. He didn't even think about it; he just accepted it. His brother had made it here, and he now understood that the man with the revolver was Filip. It had to be, though now they were about the same height, Peter and him. Peter had caught up, matching the head length that had once separated them.

Just a few days ago, Mikael thought as he stood up. He whispered, "Peter?"

Peter looked at Mikael and said, "What did you say? Did you say, Peter?"

"Yes… because it's… you?" he stammered, with a lump in his throat.

"Yes," Peter answered, and tears started rolling down his cheeks.

The wheel continued to turn, the drivers kept cracking their whips, and no one noticed what was happening up on the dock. Peter saw two strong ropes tied to a post. He was too eager to check which one was holding Mikael and Pernilla captive, so he untied both, unaware that one of the ropes led to the driven wells.

Filip knocked the man down and sat on him while tying his hands with one of the ropes from the oak.

"I don't get it," Pernilla said to herself as she ran after the three guys down the ladder.

"Hey! Don't run! Just walk slowly," Filip said, realizing that he, of all people, had to take charge. "And Peter. Stop hugging Micke and act like one of the drivers. Push him ahead of you!"

Peter understood the importance of Filip's message and forced himself to let go of Mikael. Pernilla quickly took Peter's place and pulled Mikael toward her.

"Micke! What's going on?" she whispered into Mikael's ear.

Mikael turned his face to Pernilla and said, with laughter in his throat, "It's Peter and Fille. Don't ask me what happened, but it's them. I'm sure."

"But they're… adults."

"I know. We'll figure it out later. Just go now."

They continued toward the slope, and from time to time, Filip cast a glance backward. It seemed like no one had noticed them.

After a few minutes, they reached the slope and began to climb up. Once they were far enough up to feel safe, they sat down on the grass.

Peter crouched down in front of Mikael, placed his hands on his shoulders, and said, "Can you explain this to me, Micke? We get here after ten years, and you're still only twelve."

After ten years, Mikael thought. Is he kidding, or am I dreaming?

"But we haven't even been here for two days. Me and Pernilla."

"I got here just before Mikael," Pernilla added, asking, "When did you get here?"

"Last night," Filip replied. "But how is that even possible? How can you have only been here two days? Back home, it's been ten years."

"Ten years before we got here," Peter said, looking at Filip.

"Do you get it? It had been ten years since we went through the mountain. We've been here for half a day. Micke and Pernilla have been here for almost two days. Do you get what that means?"

Filip went pale. He did the math and didn't like what he came up with. "What the hell. That must mean it's soon been at least five more years back home. Damn, Peter! We have to go back. Now, right away!"

Both Mikael and Pernilla understood what Filip had concluded and became genuinely scared. If they manage to get back, what will happen then? If they even get back! Mikael and Pernilla tried but failed, but the stone must have come through because Peter and Filip were here now. They got the letter!

"Did you get the letter?" Mikael shouted, standing up. "Peter. You got the letter. Right?"

"Yes. That's why we came here."

"I know how we'll get through. With speed. That's the only way."

Peter and Filip looked at Mikael in confusion.

"What do you mean by speed? Isn't it just a matter of returning the way we came?" Peter asked.

"We've already tried that, and it doesn't work. But the stone with the letter came through. I threw it through the mountain, and you got the letter. I even know how we should do it." He turned to Pernilla and continued, "The couch, Pernilla! Or what? We'll hang it on a rope from one of the trees above the mountain peak. That has to give a hell of a speed."

"Don't swear, Mikael!" Pernilla interrupted, giving him a sharp look while she wanted to hug him for his resourcefulness.

"The couch! What kind of couch?" Peter asked.

"You'll see later. Now we have to go. Or how many years do you want to stay here, really?"

Down at the mine, the outermost well noticed that the rope holding them captive at the oak had come loose. He carefully looked back to see if the driver was watching him. When he saw the man was a bit further away, he gently pulled the rope out of the steel rings attached to his wrists. Then, he caught the attention of the next well and showed him the end of the rope. He continued to give the wheel speed to allow more wellsts to break free.

Once enough were free, they would go to the attack.

They climbed the slope and past the hideout to grab their backpacks. They continued over the grass-covered field along the same path they had taken before, now heading in the opposite direction. After a few hundred meters, just before they reached the horse at the tree, Peter remembered what he had saved for Mikael in the backpack.

"Stop," he said, taking off his backpack. "I have something for you here, Micke."

He reached in and pulled out the Pucko he had set aside for Mikael.

"You had another one, you rascal," Filip exclaimed, chuckling.

"Correct. But this one is for Micke. I thought you might have missed the taste of chocolate after ten years. But now it's only been a couple of days, so it might not be as effective as I intended."

Mikael lit up, and a gigantic grin spread across his face. He extended his hand and said, "I've definitely missed Pucko."

He opened the bottle, smiling at his twin brother. He brought it to his lips but hesitated just before the long-awaited first sip. He thought of Pernilla. She might have missed something from home even more than he had.

He held the bottle out to her and said, "Ladies first."

Pernilla beamed and took the bottle from Mikael. "Thanks, Mikael. You're a real gentleman."

"You can call me Micke," he replied with a proud smile.

After they shared the bottle, Mikael went to Peter and gave him a hug. Only then did everything feel strange. Only now could he accept that Peter was actually an adult. Tall and a bit plump around the stomach. Ten years older than him. Very strange.

They continued the last stretch to Peter and Filip's camp. They greeted the horse and sat down in the shade. There, they rested while planning how to get back. Mikael explained his idea with the couch, the one he and Pernilla had built and hoped was still at the farm. They would find a strong rope and hang the couch in a tree. Make sure they can stretch it and then sit in it, waiting for the light in the mountain wall.

Mikael was convinced it would work. The others weren't as sure.

"What if we don't make it through? We'll probably crash into the mountain wall and get ourselves killed," Filip said. He wasn't eager to accept Mikael's idea. But with no other ideas, he was willing to give it a try.

"We have to time it perfectly," Peter said. "Get ready and wait for the light to be at its brightest. Because we probably only get one shot."

"Yes. And we'll need to think carefully when we hang the couch to make sure it hits right in the middle," Mikael concluded the discussion.

They agreed to give it a try. They couldn't think of a better idea.

They broke camp and set off. The sun was nearing the horizon, and they expected to reach the mountain by evening. They followed the gravel paths and talked about old memories from their last summer together.

An hour later, they arrived. They stopped when they saw the hill a bit ahead, and Mikael immediately began trying to locate a good tree to use for their four-person swing. He thought he spotted a perfect branch sticking out from the mountain but couldn't tell if it would work or not. He needed to get closer.

"Come on, let's give it our all for the last stretch!" he shouted, picking up speed. The others followed, eager to reach their destination as quickly as possible. They even had the horse trot the final stretch before turning off onto the field.

When they arrived, they all stood together and looked up at the trees above.

"There!" said Pernilla. "That branch must work!"

"Pernilla! You're a genius!" Mikael shouted.

"It's perfect!"

Both Peter and Filip agreed, and Filip lifted the rope from the cart and started climbing up one side of the mountain. When he reached the top, he asked which branch it was, and the unanimous answer came from below: "That one!"

He untangled the mess of rope, cut it into two equal lengths, and prepared four ends that could be tied to the swing. He then attached the middle of the rope to the tree branch and made his way back down.

When he reached the bottom, the others had already started tying the ends to the swing.

Peter, naturally the strongest of them, had lifted the swing a bit off the ground while Mikael and Pernilla tied the knots. Filip helped with the final adjustments to make sure it was as stable and secure as possible. He had also saved a piece of rope to secure the swing to the tree a little further from the mountain wall, which they would cut off when it was time to return.

Now, they sat in the swing. One after another in a line. The horse stood a little way off, head tilted, eyes fixed on the four of them.

They had drawn lots to decide their seating order. Filip had drawn the short straw and ended up at the front. Next was Pernilla, followed by Mikael and Peter.

The darkness had fallen, and they had been sitting still in the swing for a long time without anything happening, almost falling asleep, when Pernilla thought she heard a crackling sound.

Nothing was visible yet. Not a single light glimmer, just a faint, barely audible crackling. But then the sky lit up in an increasingly stronger purple color, and at once, the mountain wall was illuminated.

"It's happening," Mikael shouted, instantly wide awake. With eyes wide open, he put his arms around Pernilla and yelled: "We're going home now."

Peter was ready with the knife. The rope that had raised the swing was as taut as a piano string. He positioned the sharp edge and waited for the right moment.

"Be ready now, Peter," Filip called. "When it's at its most intense, cut the rope."

"But how will I know?" he shouted back. "I mean, how do we know when it's most intense?"

"When we all shout 'NOW' at the same time. Just be ready, and you'll know."

The mountain wall continued to shimmer and crackle, growing more powerful as time went on. The dark sky above them shone even more brightly in purple, and when they looked up, they could make out more shades in large swathes that seemed to move back and forth in blue, green, and orange.

It won't get more intense than this, Mikael thought as he sat with his gaze fixed upward, arms around Pernilla. And when he looked back down at the mountain wall, feeling the heat radiating on his face and the intense light in his eyes, he filled his lungs to the limit and yelled out: "Noooow!"

The others joined in, and Peter pulled hard with the sharp knife against the rope.

Like a cannon shot, the swing came flying toward the mountain wall. All four ducked their heads as if riding the most terrifying roller coaster at an amusement park, screaming into the air and terrified of what awaited them.

Would it stop abruptly when they hit the mountain, or would they go straight through? What would happen if they only got a little way into the mountain?

Like Pernilla's scarf?

Many eerie thoughts crossed their minds, but when they collided with the mountain wall, it felt like cycling straight into a soft bush. Mikael looked up and saw Filip and the front part of the swing sink into the mountain. He saw Pernilla's legs follow, and then everything went black.

Chapter 12

That a portal to a twin world would be found right on our planet was, of course, a huge coincidence. And that it was placed specifically in Timmerlunda forest, in the small country of Sweden, was, of course, an even greater coincidence. But that was exactly how it was. The thin boundary between one world and another, two universes so alike, yet so different.

There are those who claim that coincidences don't happen, that what happens is meant to be in some way. But surely, coincidences do happen? Otherwise, there wouldn't be a word for it!

The moment everything went black, the temperature dropped to near zero. And it was still dark, almost pitch black, when Mikael heard someone in front of him say, "Ouch."

They were lying on their side, and Mikael could feel the frost in the grass against his face. Filip, who had been sitting at the front of the sofa, had taken the hardest hit. As if he hadn't already been hurt enough on the adventure they'd been on: "Here, have another slap!"

"How are you?" Mikael asked, followed by, "And the rest of you?"

"I think it's fine but add up how much you all weigh together; that's the weight I got in my back," Filip gasped.

"Are we home, do you think?" came from the back of the sofa. They crawled out from the sofa and looked around. Mikael and Pernilla, who had been gone the longest of the four, didn't recognize their surroundings. If it was the same place they had left ten or fifteen years ago, then the trees must have grown tall by now.

Peter and Filip, who hadn't been gone as long, saw that it was indeed true.

"We're home," Filip said excitedly, turning to the others. He grabbed their hands and pulled them into a big hug.

"Yes," Mikael shouted loudly, raising his hands in the air.

Pernilla wrapped her arms around Mikael and burst into tears of joy.

Now they were there. The place where all four of them had crossed over to the other world.

Two of them were by pure accident, and for Peter and Filip, more planned and voluntary. What none of them knew was what year it was. Nor what time of year it was. None of them thought it could be midsummer due to the cold, but otherwise, it could really be any date. Frost in the grass was something they had all experienced from time to time during different seasons.

"Anyone want to guess what year it is?" Peter asked quietly and carefully as he looked at his watch. According to his wristwatch, he and Filip had only been gone for three full Earth days and five hours, which he feared was not correct.

What year they had returned to was something they had all blocked out until now. Peter received no guesses in return, but Filip said they probably needed to go into Timmerlunda to get an answer to his question. Out here in the middle of nowhere, it was almost impossible to get an answer to that question.

It was just over ten kilometers into the town, and the walk took them nearly two hours. They were mostly silent during their walk, worried but still hopeful for the news they were all waiting for.

When the gravel beneath their shoes turned to asphalt, they could see lights in the windows of the first houses they encountered as they entered Timmerlunda.

"Since it's still night, we'd better find a store or kiosk and see if there's anything there that shows what date it is," Filip suggested.

"Good idea," Mikael said tiredly, almost half-asleep as he walked, leaning against his nearly half-meter taller twin brother. Pernilla had taken hold of the other side, keeping her arm around Peter's waist in a steady grip.

They continued through their hometown, where they had all grown up, and much was just as it always had been. The houses stood where they always had. The color of the facades had been changed on some of them, but otherwise, everything looked the same.

When they passed the park in the center of town, they stopped and looked up at the hill where they had once sat and decided they would walk all the way to the horizon. Back then, it was 1977, and only now were they all back again, whatever year it could be.

From the park, they could see Evaldsson's Tobak, which had now changed its name to the center kiosk. And in the dim streetlight, they could see the newspaper headlines in the distance. Their pulse raced, and with small, staggering steps, they headed toward the fateful answer.

On the way to the kiosk, Mikael tried to calculate what year it could be. He added the time he had spent there with Peter and Filip, but everything just spun in his head, and he finally had to give up.

Then they reached the kiosk.

Hand in hand, they bent down slowly to look at the date on the newspapers, and after a few seconds, they straightened up again.

With wide eyes, Mikael said, "Oops," and after a brief pause, added, "Now I'm going to get scolded by Mom."

"1992," the others read in unison.

"Tenth of May 1992," Mikael said.

"Almost five years, Peter," Filip said.

Mikael started adding up the years, but Pernilla was quicker and exclaimed, "Fifteen years, Mikael. We've been gone for fifteen years! Do you understand?"

"Yes and no," Mikael replied. "I get it but still don't."

"I wonder what's happened to my job," Peter said quietly and carefully, looking at Filip.

"And yours? And my apartment?" Then, turning to Mikael: "And Mom and Dad! I wonder how they'll react when they see that we're alive. They definitely think you're dead, Micke, but I wonder what they think about me? Probably the same, I guess."

"They probably think we're all dead," Pernilla added, suddenly waking up from the shock. She now understood that they were actually back in Timmerlunda again, and it was only a couple of hundred meters from her home. If her parents still lived there, that is.

"I want to go home to my mom and dad," she continued, looking at the others. "Will you come with me?"

"I guess we'll have to start there," Filip said, followed by, "Maybe we can call our parents from there and ask them to come here."

"We need to figure out what to say to them. I guess it's going to be a bit of a shock for them when they see Micke and me. How suddenly there are ten years between us," Peter said.

"Everyone's going to be shocked. It'll probably take time to get used to it. No one will believe that we've been in another world, I mean," Filip said.

"Come on, let's go," Mikael said. "We'll figure something out on the way. Or we just say it as it is. Maybe that's best. Then they'll believe it or not."

"You're probably right, Micke. No point in trying to make up something else. What would it even be, in that case?" Peter said.

On their way to Pernilla's house, they passed the old school, which had been transformed into an old folks' home some time ago. Mikael and Pernilla were completely stunned when they read the sign outside, wondering where they were supposed to go to school now. Peter explained that he now lived in Rågmanstorp, or rather, had lived in Rågmanstorp. He didn't think he had his apartment anymore after five years of absence. He also explained that Timmerlunda had begun its transformation into a so-called relocation town about ten years ago.

"You'll just have to finish school in Rågmanstorp," Peter said to his younger brother.

"Okay," Mikael replied, shrugging as if it didn't matter.

They left the school behind and turned down the street where Pernilla's parents' house was. As they approached, they saw light in the kitchen window, and Pernilla spotted her mom through the window from a distance. She stopped and covered her face with her hands in an attempt to hide her tears.

Mikael put his arm around her and said, "Come on, we're with you."

The visit to Pernilla's home was overwhelming. Her mother had first thought she had seen a ghost. Partly because her daughter suddenly stood there at the door and partly because she still looked the same age as when she disappeared fifteen years ago. It only took ten seconds before she fainted for the first time that morning. Later, when Mikael, Peter, and Filip were about to leave with the twins' parents, she had already fainted three times. And on one of those occasions, she was joined by the twins' mother.

That morning was truly special. It took time, but in the end, the parents chose to accept the story given by the children. They were standing there in front of them, alive and well, all four of them healthy and fine. But somehow, it was easier to understand Peter and Filip's absence. Mikael and Pernilla, on the other hand, were still two small children and hadn't changed at all in fifteen years! It took time.

After a while, Peter and Filip moved back to Timmerlunda. There were plenty of housing options available, and the prices were low. Peter, who had gotten a job at the factory again, earned a steady salary and managed to get a loan for a down payment on an apartment in the central part of Timmerlunda. Filip, who wasn't welcome back in the military, also chose to take a job at the factory with Peter. He settled for a rental apartment on the outskirts of the town.

Mikael lived at home with his parents for a couple of months but constantly felt like something was missing. He wanted to be close to his twin brother and eventually got his parents' permission to move in with Peter. This was something Peter didn't mind, as he, too, missed being near his brother. But it wasn't just Peter that Mikael missed; he also missed Pernilla. The adventure they had been through together had bonded them like two swallows chasing the same insect. In Timmerlunda, they could meet every day, take the same bus to school, share the memories that brought them together, and just be together.

One evening, when all four of them were sitting together on the hill in the park, the hill where they often sat together in the summers—Mikael, Peter, and Filip—Filip said, "Have you thought about something? If we want, and if we dare, we could travel to the other world and stay for a few days, then come back! If we did that, we'd end up even further ahead in time!"

"What!" said the other three in unison.

"What do you mean?" Peter added.

"Think about it! If we manage to get through and stay for... let's say, three days, then come back. It would be the year twenty-two hundred twenty-two! Do you get it? Wouldn't that be cool?"

"Do you really think it would work?" said Mikael, excited.

"Please, stop now," said Pernilla. "You don't want to go back there, to the rotten world, do you?"

"Come on. Do you think the mountain will just open up because we walk up and ask it?" said Peter.

"I just don't get why you're even considering this. Why can't we just be here and now?" Pernilla snapped.

"Because we can!" said Filip, now really fired up about the idea.

"No. We stay here. I agree with Pernilla. I want to live in the moment," said Mikael, suddenly turning.

Maybe it was because of Pernilla. Maybe it was because he was tired of all the traveling. Maybe it was mostly because Pernilla thought that. If Peter and Filip wanted to "travel in time," they could do that. It might be fun to try being older than Peter for once, Mikael thought. If Peter were ten years older than he is now, Mikael would be at least twenty years older than Peter and Filip if they decided to be gone for three of the other world's days.

"Are you in, Peter?" Filip asked, now fully on board with the idea.

"Eh. I don't know. Maybe it's best to stay here after all. Who knows what kind of mess we'll cause if we end up there again? And I'm not exactly eager to run into the monsters again."

"Scaredy-cat."

"...you can be your own..." Peter finished, shoving Filip so he fell over.

They decided not to go back to the mountain wall anymore, afraid of what might happen. One visit to that world was enough. More than enough. That's what they decided at that moment.

Just that evening...

The Second Journey

Chapter 13

Peter grabbed a cinnamon bun and a Swedish punsch roll and placed them on the plate. He slid the tray along the wooden counter towards the cash register. At the same time, he scanned the café's messy furnishings in search of Filip, who was supposed to meet him.

It had been five months since all four of them had sat up on the hill together. It had been summer then, but now winter was approaching, and outside the café, the snow was gently falling from a gray sky. Mikael was still living at Peter's house, and everything was going well. At least outwardly.

For the past month, Peter had felt that something wasn't right. That something wasn't as it should be. He had managed to hide his worry from Mikael and hadn't talked to anyone about it. In the beginning, he didn't understand what it was, but after a while, it became clear to him. It was the age difference. The age difference between him and Mikael. It just didn't feel right.

He spotted Filip at the far corner, behind a bookshelf protruding from the wall, filled to the brim with books of various sizes.

Good, Peter thought. Then, we can sit undisturbed.

He weaved his way between tables and chairs, once again thinking about how he would present the idea to Filip. For a week now, he had been thinking about it, the idea he was about to present to him. He had no idea how Filip would react. Either he'd be 'in', or he wouldn't. That's how it was with Filip. No gray area.

"There you are," Peter said to Filip as he rounded the bookshelf.

Filip sat with a book in hand and was already on the second chapter. "So, now you show up?"

"Sorry. I drove Micke to soccer practice and got stuck for a while. But better late than never. Right?"

Peter set the tray down on the table, and Filip closed the book.

"Terribly boring book. I can't understand how I managed to read the whole first chapter," said Filip, pushing the book between two world atlases.

"Have you ever managed to read an entire book?" Peter asked sarcastically, extending the plate of treats towards Filip. "Pick whichever you want."

Filip immediately grabbed the punsch roll and broke it in half. He shoved one half into his mouth, and the other he placed back on the plate. "One-half is enough. I have to think about my figure, you know."

"Ha, ha, ha," Peter chuckled. "You've never done that before. Why start now?"

"Better late than never, as you said."

Peter looked into Filip's eyes and became a bit more serious, preparing to tell Filip how he was feeling.

Filip noticed Peter's change in tone and decided to remain silent. He understood Peter wanted to tell him something.

Peter lifted the cinnamon bun to his mouth but paused and put it back on the plate. "You, Filip. There's something I need to talk to you about."

"Okay. What's that?" Filip asked calmly and slowly.

"It's about the age difference between me and Micke. It doesn't feel right. I don't know how Micke feels, but maybe he feels the same way. I have no idea, haven't even dared to ask. I don't feel good about it. It feels really tough."

"Okay."

"So… I've been thinking about something and wanted to see what you think of it."

Peter took a deep breath and continued.

"This summer, when we sat up on the hill in the park, you had an idea. That we should get back to the other world. Do you remember that?"

"Yeah, but no one seemed up for it, so we dropped it. Right? That's how it was, wasn't it?"

"Yeah. But your idea was that we should stay together for several days, all of us. What I'm thinking now is that just you and I go, and we stay just long enough for Micke to catch up with us."

He locked eyes with Filip to try to gauge his reaction. Filip's eyes were serious at first, and Peter could tell he was thinking. Then he saw his mouth change shape slightly, followed by his eyes relaxing, and finally, a small grin that grew on his face.

"Of course, I'm in."

"Are you? Completely sure?"

"Yeah, we can at least give it a shot. It's not guaranteed we'll even make it there. Maybe we just got lucky last time. No idea."

"I think I have an idea. A hint, at least. I've checked it out a bit. Do you remember when we crossed over? There was unusually high solar activity, then? We talked about it. Do you remember?"

"Yeah, I remember. Do you think it has something to do with it?"

"I think so. I remember the night after Micke disappeared when we were looking for him. Do you remember the night sky then? It was completely purple and weird. Just like it was the night we crossed over, you and I."

"Yeah, that's true."

"And do you know what I heard on the news yesterday?"

"No, but I can guess. Unusually high solar activity."

"Yep."

"So, what do you think it is that allowed us to get to another world? Do you think it's one of those wormholes astronomers talk about?"

"Maybe a wormhole. Or something else. I think it feels like physicists and others just guess. But I don't know. Yeah, maybe a wormhole. But something I think could be connected is the solar activity if you think about how it was in the other world, with the giant sun. I've read that our sun will also grow huge in a few million years, or was it billions of years, I can't quite remember. But anyway, on the other side, it's probably always super high solar activity. You remember the lead suits."

"And the lead hats," Filip interjected.

"Exactly. They were supposed to protect us from radiation," Peter said, now picking up the cinnamon bun again from the plate. He broke it in half and took a bite of one half.

"Maybe the mountain in the other world opens up every day, now and then."

"That's what I'm hoping for," Peter said between bites. He swallowed and continued, "We need to figure out exactly when we're going back. We should have one full day, maximum, I guess. But we'll figure that out later. I get that we won't hit the exact right age, but we have to try to get as close as possible."

"And we absolutely can't get stuck there!"

"I'm thinking we'll bring food and water and stay near the mountain at all times. Just to be safe."

"You've already planned everything down to the smallest detail," Filip said, gobbling up the second half of the bun.

"Yeah, I've been thinking about it for a while, as you might guess."

"We'll make it work, Peter. Of course, we need to be the same age, all three of us, or it would be totally ridiculous."

"All four," Peter corrected.

"Yeah, of course. Pernilla, too."

"I think Micke's in love."

"Ha, ha. The little rascal. We'll see when we come back in ten years. Maybe you'll be Uncle Peter."

"Yeah, who knows? Maybe."

Peter and Filip left the café together. Outside, the snowfall had increased in intensity, and it had started to get a little darker. It was only half past five. It was clear winter was on its way.

They had decided to make their attempt this weekend. The news had predicted the sun's activities would peak on Saturday. And already today, with clear weather, it would be possible to see a fantastic night sky with the northern lights reaching far down into southern Sweden, they had said.

Peter had been thinking about whether he should tell Mikael about his plan. He at least wanted to say goodbye to Mikael in case something went wrong. He had decided to tell him that he and Filip were going on a charter vacation and that he would need to stay at his parents' house during that time. Then he would write a letter and leave it in the apartment with an explanation, saying that he and Filip were heading to the other world. Peter hoped he would understand.

It was lunchtime at the factory, and Peter and Filip went out for a walk after they emptied their lunch boxes.

"Macaroni and sausage for three days in a row now," Filip said with disdain. "I need to expand my lunch repertoire."

"Ah, you just need to mix it up a bit. Meatballs, fish sticks, meat patties. Most things go with pasta. Just toss in some vegetables, and it'll be fine."

"Speaking of food. What are we bringing? And how long will we stay over there?"

"I've actually calculated it now. You'll have to help think so we don't mess it up."

"Okay. Let's hear it."

Peter pulled a piece of paper from his back pocket and thought for a moment. Then he said, "As I remember, it was one in the morning when we crossed over to the other world last time, and when we came back, my clock showed that it had been three days and five hours. Then, almost exactly five years had passed here at home, almost to the month or so. Doesn't that seem to fit?"

"Yeah... I think so."

"That means we need to be gone twice as long: six Earth days and ten hours. At least as close as possible. We'll need to keep an eye on my clock," Peter said, holding it out to Filip.

"Then we'll need to make sure it's accurate and that you don't lose it when we're there. However, I could also bring a clock. The only problem is, I don't have one. I guess I'll just buy one for safety's sake."

"I think you should do that. And one of good quality. I got mine when I turned twenty. It's a self-winding clock. That means there's no battery that can run out. Buy a good quality clock for safety. We probably shouldn't rely on just one."

"Then, food. It worked to eat from the ax, but I got tired of it pretty quickly. It'd be good to bring something else, too," Filip said, sticking out his tongue.

"Mm. Food for six days. That's quite a lot."

"I've got an idea. How about macaroni? Then we'll bring a portable stove too. There's water over there."

"Ha, ha. Yeah, of course, you want macaroni. That works. We'll go with that. And loads of sausage."

They returned from the walk after half an hour and went back to the department where they worked. Outside, it was cold, but inside the factory, it was warm and cozy. It was

Thursday, and soon it would be the weekend. They were going to have everything ready by then. The final planning would be done on Friday night after Peter dropped off Mikael at his parents' house after he said goodbye to Mikael.

Peter stuffed the last things into his backpack and began putting on his outer clothes. Filip was about to arrive any minute, and they had agreed to meet outside Peter's apartment. One of the items Peter had packed was the lead suit. He had kept it mostly as a souvenir, but now it would come in handy again. Filip had done the same.

They met up in the parking lot outside and set off, and after a half-hour walk, they passed the lake, which would soon get its first layer of ice for the season. It was early afternoon, and they expected to be at the mountain before it got dark. They also expected the mountain to open up tonight, or at least that night, since solar activity would peak that day.

They were mostly silent as they trudged along the road to the mountain. They could feel the cold setting in, and they wanted to keep up a fast pace to stay warm. After just a couple of hours, they arrived.

"Look here. The sofa's still here. Looks like no one's been here after all," said Filip, setting down his backpack.

"Right. You got the rope?"

"Yep," Filip said, kicking his backpack to show that it was inside.

They planned to use the rope for the return trip. They would tie it high up in a tree above the mountain ridge and swing back. A bit like last time, but this time without the sofa.

"Okay, now we just have to wait. But it's probably best to try and get a fire going right away. It's going to get really cold."

They gathered some dry twigs and got a fire going almost at once. Filip took out a pack of sausages and skewered one on a stick.

"Look up," said Peter.

"Wow. What colors."

The sky crackled with the most amazing colors, and it seemed to dance in the dark sky. In a couple of hours, the background would be completely black, and the contrasts would be even clearer. They had a fantastic night ahead, no matter how long it would turn out to be.

"I wish Micke were here. I already miss him."

"Well, we'll be back soon."

"Yes, we will. But think about Micke. For him, it will take ten years before we come back."

"Yeah, it sure feels good to get a little revenge," said Filip jokingly, smiling at Peter.

"Ha, ha," replied Peter, thinking about how Mikael would react when he read the letter.

Ten years is a long time at that age. It's the entire middle school, three years of high school, and then a couple of years of working. Peter knew how slowly time goes when you miss your best friend, your brother. Your twin. He wondered if he was selfish for leaving like this. He didn't know how Mikael felt, if he felt the same way about the age gap. He decided that he could be a little selfish this time.

In another world, both close and far from ours, a rebellion of unprecedented scale was taking place. Just a couple of hours after the four had re-entered the Timmerlunda world, the wellsts began to break free from the drill wheel because one of the four, a bit clumsily, had untied not only the rope that Mikael and Pernilla had been fastened to but also the rope that held the wellsts fast to the spokes.

The nearest wellst had seen the loose rope and alerted the next wellst inside. Slowly, it pulled the rope out of the iron rings that held it to the spoke and waited until the ones closest inside were also free. At a given moment, they overwhelmed the drivers behind them and then helped the other wellsts break free.

As more and more wellsts were freed from their reins, the drivers and guards at their spokes were neutralized one by one. They then moved on to the next spoke, where they helped others escape. Chaos erupted, which was difficult to grasp for the remaining guards, and shortly after, they were defeated one by one. When the last man was neutralized, the group continued in a large mass toward the factory area, where they ran riot inside the four walls.

The people who came in their way wished they had been anywhere else. The vengeful monsters showed why it was legitimate to call them monsters. With blows, bites, and roars, they made their way forward, leaving only chunks of flesh and death behind. When they stopped and saw the devastation they had left behind, they united in a collective scream that could be heard all the way to the village, where the now fatherless children and newly widowed women would have to face the attack that awaited them. For now, they wanted to return to the world from which they had been so mercilessly taken.

But not all of them.

A small group of four decided to stay behind to see if they could create a decent life in this world. At least give it a chance. This group set off toward the place where Peter and Filip would soon be. The two would experience a journey that would prove to be utterly insane and not at all as easy and smooth as they had imagined.

Chapter 14

"Maybe it's time to turn the sausage's," Filip said to Peter, who had been lost in thought and had completely forgotten about the sausage's, which was now pitch black.

"Oops," Peter said, quickly pulling the sausage up while hearing a crackling sound that didn't come from the fire. "Filip. Did you hear that?"

"I heard. Maybe it's time?"

"Seems like it. We better get ready," Peter replied, stuffing the entire sausage into his mouth and feeling his pulse race.

The crackling grew louder, and soon, they saw the glow grow stronger at the bottom of the hill. They hurried to get their things into their backpacks and grabbed the large cloth bags they'd filled with supplies. Side by side, they stood ready to step into the parallel world. They could feel the pull, the tugging at them. The rock wall was now fully illuminated, and the deafening crackling drowned out all other sounds around them.

"Peter, it's happening now. Are you ready?"

"No. Are you?"

"No, but I probably never will be, so there's no point in holding back. No use in resisting anymore."

They let go and allowed themselves to be pulled into the glow. They first felt the bags lift from the ground, and they had to hold on with all their might to avoid losing their grip. The moment after, they were pulled in with a force strong enough to move mountains, and just a fraction of a second later, they fell into the other world in a heap of bags, backpacks, arms, and legs. They opened their eyes and, to their horror, saw four figures speeding toward their location.

"Shit, Peter. We need to go. Fast."

The monsters hadn't spotted them yet. As they walked along the gravel path, they noticed the glow from the mountain and started heading toward it just before Peter and Filip crossed over. Now, they were partially hidden by the tall grass, and Peter and Filip saw their chance to escape. They also had the blindingly bright glow from the mountain to thank, as it made them harder to spot. If they had waited just a few seconds longer before allowing themselves to be sucked in, they would have ended up neatly laid out on a — for the monsters — well-set buffet.

They quickly moved away from the location and took cover behind a large tree beside the hill.

"Now we're damn quiet," Filip whispered to Peter.

Their hearts were racing at full speed, and their breathing was heavy. They were afraid that would be enough to get them noticed by the monsters.

The creatures hadn't reached the mountain yet, and they now saw that the brightness was starting to fade. The crackling decreased, and after only a few seconds, it went completely silent. Now, it was as dark as the grave again.

"Are they coming this way?" Peter whispered.

"I think so. But if we just stay completely still, maybe they'll leave now that the mountain's gone dark. Now we're completely silent."

After only a few seconds, the monsters reached the side of them, and they realized that if they made it out alive now, they had the darkness to thank.

Peter and Filip continued to lie completely still. The monsters grunted something, and they were now only four or five meters away from them. They heard one of them inhale through its nostrils as if it had caught a scent. Was it theirs?

They slowly started moving away in the opposite direction, away from Peter and Filip. Peter let out a quiet breath and hoped they were around.

Filip, who wasn't as sure they wouldn't turn back, gently reached into his backpack and pulled out the revolver he had kept since their last visit. He silently opened the cylinder to make sure there were still rounds inside. He counted to four. Half full. Should he dare look for more in his backpack or rely on his accuracy?

He decided on the latter. He couldn't risk being spotted.

Just as they were sure they wouldn't be discovered, one of the monsters came walking directly toward them. Filip tightened the cock. Peter slowly sat up in a starting position as if preparing for a hundred-meter sprint. If any of them came close, he would take off and run. That was at least his plan at the moment. But when the monster lunged at them and Filip fired the revolver, he froze. Life played out in ultra-slow motion, and Mikael was the main character in every scene.

The well-monster landed directly over him after Filip had hit a bullseye right in the chest.

Then, the other three came charging toward them. Filip prepared himself while Peter shoved the dead, hairy, foul-smelling monster aside.

"Run," Filip shouted, standing in front of Peter.

"What?" Peter managed to answer before the next shot was fired.

The bullet turned the well-monster's right ear into mush and then continued its path toward the next one, which dropped to its knees.

The bullet had hit right in one of its eyes.

"Run, I said," Filip shouted loudly.

Filip was ready to sacrifice his life for Peter. Right now, the priority was for Peter to survive and be reunited with his brother. Peter didn't have much to contribute. Filip had the revolver — what did Peter have to fight with? At best, some cans of Bullens Pilsner sausages! Filip was trained for situations like this; Peter was not. Peter's survival was the highest priority. He had to reunite with his brother again, no matter what the cost.

Peter took off with the backpack on his back. He had to leave the food bag behind. Filip fired the revolver at the monster with the smashed ear, causing it to fall to the side. The other well-monster, the one that had just had its eyes reduced to one, fell into the tall grass with its arms stretched out straight ahead in one last attempt to reach Filip. But then it just lay still.

One left, Filip thought, before the well-monster with one ear got back up after being struck by the revolver.

"Okay, two then," he yelled and raised the revolver, firing again.

This time, he made a perfect shot. The monster fell flat on the ground, and Filip now knew he had only one shot left.

The last well-monster hesitated for a fraction of a second, turned around, and then sped off toward the field at high speed.

Everything happened so quickly that Filip didn't have time to think. Above all, he wanted to put a bullet in the last one, too. Now that it was fleeing, they couldn't relax for a second. They would always have to keep looking over their shoulders, nervous and anxious that it would attack without warning.

Filip heard a sound behind him. He slowly turned his head and moved the revolver in the same motion.

Now my final moment has come, he thought, before he saw what had sneaked up behind him. There stood Peter, with a large stone in each hand, ready to attack.

"Shit, Peter, you scared me," he exhaled.

"Are they all dead? How many were there?"

"One got away. I don't know exactly where it is, but we have to be careful. We can't relax just yet."

"Where did it go?"

"Out to the field. I'm hoping it ran off and won't come back. It seems like it's the last one now. But as I said, we can't relax yet; we have to keep an eye out at all times."

"We're leaving," Peter said, grabbing the bags. "I'll carry it so you can be ready with the gun."

"The revolver. It's called the revolver."

"Never mind. Just make sure it's fully loaded."

Filip reloaded the revolver and followed Peter along the edge between the field and the mountain wall, heading in the opposite direction from the monster's escape route. Slowly, they approached the unexplored ground.

They walked until it started to get light. It was warm even though it was night, and the heavy lead clothing hadn't made things any better. Peter checked his watch when he saw the first rays of sunlight in the sky and could confirm that they had been walking for over eight hours.

Twice, they had stopped to eat, and as time passed, they became more and more relaxed. They realized that the well-armed men were not after them, and after a while, Filip had put the revolver away and helped Peter with one of the food bags.

Now that it was lighter, they saw that the landscape ahead looked different from the areas they had been in before. The mountain lay in the daylight and was a little hilly. It was a little bit like along the west coast, where Peter and Mikael had spent a few weeks one summer long ago. They were only ten years old then, but Peter remembered it as if it was yesterday.

***

Their parents had borrowed a caravan from a colleague. The journey had taken them through almost half of Sweden, and it had felt like they would never arrive. But in the end, they did. They stayed at a campsite right next to the sea. The weather was fine, warm and pleasant, and the sea was salty, not like the sea they were used to swimming in, the brackish, almost salt-free water far up in the Bay of Bothnia.

As soon as they got out of the car, they ran down along the rocks toward the water. Each of them had a string with a clothespin tied at the end. They were going to fish for crabs. They had heard from a classmate who had been there before that this was what you did on the west coast.

Sitting on separate stones with their feet and clothespins in the water, they waited for the big catch. The mussel clamped into the clothespin, which they had smashed between two stones.

"Look, Peter," Mikael shouted, pointing down into the water.

Peter quickly pulled his feet out of the water. "I see. A big one."

The crab, which wasn't actually very large, clamped one of its claws into Mikael's mussel. Mikael pulled it up and let out a joyful shout.

Even today, Peter remembers Mikael's cheerful mood that summer, just like all the summers and the time in between. Mikael was usually happy. Even when he should have been sad, something Peter never really understood. Even though they had been apart for only a day, Peter had already missed him. He hoped time would go quickly, he thought. But only eight, ten hours had passed since they 'went through' the mountain. That meant they still had six full days ahead of them, which, in turn, meant almost a whole day here in this world.

Peter sat down on a rock and told Filip they needed to rest for a bit.

"It looks different here," said Filip.

"Yeah, a bit like the west coast. Have you been there?"

"No, never. I haven't been further south than Stockholm."

"Maybe we should stay here until it's time to head back. I see there's a stream ahead, too. So, we have water."

Filip squinted his eyes and said, "Looks like it ran into a hole in the mountain. Should we go check it out?"

They walked the short distance to the stream, and sure enough, the water disappeared into a hole in the mountain.

"Strange," said Peter. "We need to explore this more. At least it will pass the time."

They took a stone and dropped it into the hole, counting the seconds.

"One, two..."

Plop!

"It seems like there's a whole lake down there," exclaimed Filip. "And not so far down."

"Do you think we can go down?"

"Maybe. But not here; the hole is too narrow."

They walked around, looking for a larger hole, and when they reached the other side of the hill, they saw what looked like some sort of entrance into the mountain. It was definitely something built by humans. Not something nature had made itself.

Large stones had been stacked against the mountain. They followed the path and came to the opening, which was large enough for them to walk straight through.

"Shall we?" Peter asked.

"Of course. Seems completely harmless."

Filip pulled a flashlight from his pack, and then they entered the darkness. The passage led straight ahead for a bit, then turned left toward a staircase. From the stairs, they could hear the water rushing down the mountain, down into the underground lake they had previously guessed would be there.

They went deeper and deeper, reaching a landing where a staircase split to the right and left. They heard the sound of water coming from the right and decided to take that staircase.

When they got down, they saw that the light from the hole where the water flowed down illuminated the entire underground lake. The lake, which was more like a large pond, sparkled in the light.

"Looks really cozy," said Filip. "Maybe we can spend the day here?"

"So, we don't have to wear these," Peter replied, throwing off his lead suit.

It was like a big underground room down there, and a small staircase led down to the water from the landing where they stood.

"Perfect spot. We can lie here and relax until it's time to go back. Maybe even take a dip. What do you think, Peter?"

"As long as the water isn't too cold."

"I don't think it is. It's warm and comfortable here anyway. The water should be warm too," Filip thought, now having taken off both his backpack, lead suit, and the t-shirt he wore underneath.

"We'll go down and check," Peter said, beginning to walk down the stairs.

The water was warm enough, and it felt nice to cool off from the hike. They swam for a while and then sat on the lowest step with their feet in the water.

Peter's thoughts immediately returned to the crab fishing that summer long ago, but he was quickly awakened by sounds from the stairs above.

Sounds coming toward them.

At home, life continued. It had soon been a year since Peter and Filip set off. Mikael had read the letter Peter left for him and had initially become a bit sad and worried. Sad because he wouldn't get to see him for ten years and worried that he might never come back at all. But after letting it sink in, he understood his brother, and he felt at ease knowing Filip was with him. Filip, who had saved both him and Peter so many times before. With Filip, he felt safe.

Peter lifted his feet out of the water, turned around, and saw two people coming down the stairs. It was dark in that direction, but he thought he could see that they were two shorter individuals, perhaps children.

They quickly stood up and put on their pants and shirts. Their packs were still up on the landing, and they realized they wouldn't make it there before the people reached the bottom.

Maybe they were coming down here to swim?

Where were they coming from, then?

They decided to stay where they were. They probably didn't need to worry about being attacked, at least not if they were children. They would probably be more scared of Peter and Filip.

They stood off to the side of the stairs and waited for them. When the children reached the last steps, they saw Peter and Filip and froze. They screamed and quickly disappeared back up the stairs. They seemed utterly terrified.

"Come on, let's follow and see where they go," said Filip, pulling on Peter's arm.

They saw that the children had placed a lamp a little higher up, and in its light, they could see well enough to follow them from a distance.

They continued up the stairs the same way they had come, but where it split, the children went the other way, down the stairs, deeper into the mountain.

"They didn't come from outside," Peter said, surprised, looking at Filip. "Should we follow them?"

"They might be going to get someone. Maybe their parents?"

"I think we should follow them. Let's get our stuff first. What can happen? They weren't monster creatures from what I saw."

Filip reluctantly agreed but didn't say anything about it.

After they went back down to the landing to put on their shoes and clothes, they went up again to take the stairs down into the mountain. They didn't hear any sounds from below yet, but it felt a little creepy. They stayed close together and tried not to shine the flashlight too far down.

They didn't want to give away their position too soon if someone was coming their way.

After they came down the stairs, they continued along the passage until they reached a wooden door. They walked up to the door and pulled lightly on the handle. At the same moment, the door opened from the inside, and to their surprise, they came face-to-face with two older men. Both the men and Peter and Filip screamed in surprise at the unexpected meeting. Not out of fear but more from the unexpected situation.

Filip raised his hands to show he was harmless and didn't mean anyone any harm. Peter looked at Filip and did the same. The men went silent and looked at each other before one of them said something neither Peter nor Filip understood.

"Hello," said Filip in an attempt to be friendly. Then he extended his hand.

Peter was surprised when one of the men reached out his hand to return the greeting. The man even smiled.

Filip mimed swimming with his arms and then pointed toward the stairs. He thought the men understood because they smiled at Filip and mimicked his arm gestures.

After that successful meeting with the underground people, they were invited into their dwelling. They walked through small tunnels, and here and there, channels from the mountain above-allowed light and air to enter.

After a while, they realized it was like a small community down there. They passed through large open halls where people shared space. Some of the halls had long tables and chairs, while others were more like dormitories. They peeked into one of the smaller rooms and immediately smelled food. Peter could feel his mouth-watering, which one of the men noticed. They were at once invited to eat.

As they sat there eating, curious children and women came up to them. Peter pulled out a tin of sausages and offered it. At first, they were cautious, but once they tasted the incredibly good sausages, they wanted more.

It was unbelievable that they had found the entrance to the mountain and met these wonderful people. They lived down here, free from the heavy lead suits. Digging into the mountain like this must have taken several hundred years, Peter guessed. It must have been passed down through several generations.

It turned out that the entrance to the mountain Peter and Filip had found was rarely used. It was more of a backdoor in and out of the mountain. The main entrance was grander and was guarded day and night by a small army of both men and women.

Outside the main entrance of the mountain, farmland spread out. That's where everything needed to sustain an underground community of over two hundred people was growing. Water was supplied by the stream that ran into the mountain, and it was apparently not very popular for anyone to swim in it. Something both of them learned later that day when they showed with swimming gestures that they wanted to go back to the lake for a swim.

Another thing they experienced was that when Peter was standing there taking his swimming strokes, he realized that his watch was missing. He nearly panicked and tried to explain to the men that his watch was gone and that he had probably lost it in the lake. But the men refused to let them go back. Instead, they tried to push a strange wooden ball-like object with small holes in it towards him. Peter didn't understand anything and handed it back. From then on, they had to rely on Filip's watch.

"You guard that with your life from now on," Peter said to Filip, trying to sound authoritative.

"Aye, aye, captain," Filip responded.

They wanted to pass the time and asked the men if they could help out in the field. Amazingly, they understood what they meant and showed them the way out through the main gate. After changing into lead clothes, they followed another pair out toward the fields. They had both a hoe and a rake with them, and when they had gone some distance, the couple showed them what needed to be done. Weed removal might not have been their favorite task, but at least it passed the time.

The sun had now risen higher in the sky, and it was noticeable. It was getting warmer with each passing minute, and the thought crossed their minds that they could sneak away to the other entrance to take a dip. But they changed their minds when they spotted a well-armed figure at the end of the field.

It was a few hundred meters away, and Filip and Peter were the only ones still out in the field. They saw how it crouched down and fixed its gaze on them. Peter looked toward the main gate and estimated that it was at least two hundred meters away.

"What do we do?" Peter asked. "You didn't bring the revolver, did you?"

"No," Filip answered briefly, his mind working overtime. He tried to analyze the terrain to see if there was a good spot that could give them an advantage if the creature decided to attack.

"Think!" Peter whispered to Filip.

"Quiet, I'm thinking," came the reply.

"Good. Do it quickly because now it's coming toward us."

The creature began moving slowly in their direction. Peter wondered if it could be the same one that had escaped earlier in the morning. If it was, it was probably quite angry.

Now, it quickened its pace.

"Follow me," Filip shouted. "Grab the hoe."

Peter grabbed the hoe and took off after Filip, who had apparently spotted something. They ran as fast as the heavy clothes allowed, which wasn't very fast. The creature, however, had picked up considerably more speed and would be upon them in less than a minute.

"Up here," Filip yelled.

The field was bordered by the west coast cliffs, and at the top of one of the cliffs stood a gigantic standing stone. That was where Filip was aiming.

"What are you thinking now?" Peter asked when they reached the stone.

"We have to get up here. It's our only chance."

The creature was now halfway there.

"On my shoulders. Quickly," Filip shouted.

Peter first threw the hoe onto the stone. Then he had a quick thought that maybe this wasn't such a smart move. If they couldn't make it up, they would be left without a weapon to defend themselves with.

Filip bent down, and Peter stepped onto Filip's shoulders, using the stone for support. With a strong push, Filip stood up. With Filip pressing first on Peter's backside and then grabbing Peter's feet, Peter barely managed to get onto the stone.

"And now what?" Peter shouted from the top of the stone.

"Stay there."

Peter stood on the stone and saw Filip take off his watch. He slid it onto the rake and lifted it toward Peter.

"Take it. Quickly."

"But what about you?"

"Just take it. And if the creature comes, hit it as hard as you can with the hoe. Hide the hoe first. Try to surprise it."

"BUT WHAT ABOUT YOU?" Peter yelled, now thoroughly angry at Filip.

Filip stood still below the stone for a brief moment, looking up at Peter. Then he turned around and made his way.

Toward the creature.

Chapter 15

One of the guards outside the gate to the mountain saw Peter and Filip suddenly start running. At first, he didn't understand what they were doing.

Are they running away? From what? From us? How crazy are they, really?

Then he saw the wellst. He immediately sounded the alarm to the other guards, who gathered below the wall in front of the gate. While the guard team mobilized, he continued keeping watch. He saw one of them manage to climb onto a stone, and shortly after, the other man started running toward the wellst. Keeping the team updated, he shouted for them to intervene as one of the men approached the wellst. The guard team set off.

Armed with the strangest assortment of items and some farming tools, they hurried across the field. If Peter and Filip had run slowly, the guard team moved at a snail's pace in comparison. Peter dropped to his knees, watching as Filip ran straight at the monster with determination. He noticed the guard team approaching from the side, but only in the periphery. His gaze was locked on Filip. He felt anger boiling inside him and tried to shout, but no sound came out. The words got stuck in his throat.

What the hell are you doing? Turn back! It will kill you! YOU DAMN IDIOT!

Then came the tears. The anger gave way to despair. He had known all along that this wouldn't end well. The monster would crush Filip. This might be the last time he saw him alive. Peter lifted his wrist and saw Filip's watch. *He gave me the watch.* The realization struck him—Filip had never planned to climb onto the stone. But why run straight at the monster?

He wiped away his tears and saw Filip reach the wellst. Filip swung the steel rake from the side, striking the wellst's leg and causing it to stumble. He took another swing, aiming for the monster's neck. The monster raised its hand and caught the rake just before impact. Then, it struck.

Filip crumpled to the ground as the wellst's powerful, evil fist smashed across his neck. The monster then struck again, this time using the rake against Filip's body. The wellst stood up and let out a roar before slowly turning its gaze toward Peter.

Now everything broke loose.

Peter screamed, his rage directed at both Filip and the monster. At Filip for being such an idiot, thinking he could stand a chance against a much larger and stronger foe. And at the wellst for likely killing his best friend. Hatred grew inside him. So did courage. And revenge. He tightened his grip on the sharp steel hoe, keeping it hidden behind him as the wellst approached. He was ready to swing in a deadly arc, aiming for the monster's head.

The guard team saw the wellst moving toward the man on the tall stone but decided to focus on the downed man first. When they reached Filip, they saw blood pouring from his neck and body. The clumsiness they had shown earlier was gone—now they moved with speed and precision. They worked quickly to stop the bleeding, then lifted Filip and rushed him back to the mountain for medical care. If he survived, it would be thanks to their swift actions.

The wellst reached the stone and stopped. Peter stood firm, locking eyes with the monster, his gaze full of hatred. His body trembled with anger. He tightened his grip on the hoe, ready for revenge. Then he noticed something—the monster's ear. Or rather, the absence of one. Dried blood covered the wellst's chest.

It wasn't the monster they had seen escape.

It was the wellst they thought they had killed.

That meant there were at least two of them. And one stood right in front of him. The pressure mounted. He had to kill this one before the other came after him. He swung. Just as the monster reached up toward Peter, the hoe came crashing down with violent force. It sliced through the monster's neck, lodged into a crack in the stone, and got stuck. The metallic clang echoed all the way to the guard team, now inside the protective walls with Filip. The monster thrashed below in its death throes. Then, it stopped moving.

Peter had reduced the number of monsters by one. But at least one more was still out there. And he had no idea how Filip was doing. In that moment, Filip was like Schrödinger's Cat—both dead and alive at the same time.

Filip had lost a lot of blood by the time they carried him into the mountain's medical station. But he was alive. The wellst's sharp claws had torn a deep wound into his neck, dangerously close to the carotid artery. The steel rake had gone deep into his chest, breaking two ribs and nearly puncturing his heart. One of the rake's sharp spikes had stopped a mere millimeter from certain death.

Unconscious, Filip dreamt.

He was walking alone on a gravel road in the middle of summer. He wasn't just alone on the road—he was alone in life. He didn't understand why, but the absence of his best friends weighed on him.

Will I never see them again? Where am I going?

Slowly, memories returned. They had left him. No, they had saved him. The twins had hidden him to protect him from evil. And they had paid with their lives. That was why he was alone.

He cried as he trudged down the road, dragging his feet through the dry, dusty gravel. He looked down at his bare feet, seeing them sink deeper with each step. Soon, they were completely buried. He stopped, afraid that if he kept moving, he would disappear entirely into the dust.

Then he saw them.

Two silhouettes stood before him. Two shapeless shadows. Then they were gone. And he was alone again.

He cursed Peter and Mikael for giving their lives for him. *Why was my life worth more than theirs?* The crying persisted as he drifted back to consciousness. He cautiously opened his eyes, staring at the gray ceiling through his tears.

He scanned the room—he was inside the mountain. *How did I get here?* People surrounded him, dressed in what looked like medical clothes. One of them stood beside him, holding a small cup. They poured its contents into his open wound. Filip saw it bubble and fizz as it made contact with his torn flesh. The pain was indescribable. He blacked out again, back on the gravel road.

Peter forced himself down from the stone and started walking toward the mountain. The wellst had stopped moving. A trickle of blood ran down the rock, pooling beside it. He was certain it was dead this time. But was the other wellst nearby? His stomach churned with nerves. He quickened his pace, glancing around anxiously.

He had seen the guards carry Filip away. He had no hope that his friend was still alive.

He felt utterly alone.

Damn it, damn Filip.

When he reached the high wall, the guards let him inside the courtyard. They touched him, speaking words he didn't understand. They pulled at him, eager to get him through the main gate. Once inside, they helped him remove his outer clothes and led him to the medical station. One of them went inside and returned shortly after, signaling that he could enter. They nudged him forward.

Peter stepped into the room. In the center, on a bed, lay Filip—flat on his back, hands resting on his stomach.

He's dead, Peter thought.

Then Filip's head turned toward him.

To Filip, Peter was just an empty silhouette. Blinded by the light from the doorway, Peter looked like a shadow. But Filip knew—it was Peter.

A living Peter. In a faint voice, Filip said, "Did you get him?"

Peter felt his legs give way beneath him, but he managed to stop the fall by grabbing hold of the doorframe.

"You're alive! I was sure you were dead."

Barely audible: "I feel almost dead, you should know. But at least it's not bleeding anymore."

Peter regained control of his body and walked over to the bed. He crouched down to hear what Filip had to say.

"Did you get it?"

"Yes, but I think there's one still out there somewhere. I thought you were dead. What were you thinking?"

"I don't know... can't go on..."

He fainted again.

Peter stayed by his side for a long time. Occasionally, he was told to leave the room to eat, but there was no appetite. He could barely manage some water and bread, just enough to keep hunger at bay.

Filip woke up and faded in and out.

Peter managed to feed Filip some soup now and then, but the meager spoons of food felt insignificant. Yet, it was enough to provide him with life-sustaining energy.

When Peter wasn't with Filip, he wandered around in a daze. His thoughts wouldn't settle, and he had no sense of time or place. He often got lost inside the mountain and sometimes had to ask someone, using sign language, to guide him back to the room where Filip lay.

Peter had no idea how long they had been there until Filip took command again. As Filip recovered, Peter seemed to lose more of himself. Filip noticed Peter becoming more withdrawn and unfocused, which gave him the strength to heal and refocus on getting them back. The wounds caused by the monster on his body healed surprisingly well, and after what seemed like three or four days at home, he was healed enough to sit up in bed.

"Do you have any idea what time it is?" Filip asked. "How long have I been lying here?"

Peter was momentarily thrown off. Time? He had completely lost track of it. His only thoughts had been about when Filip would recover. Every time he entered the room, he hoped Filip would be healthy and cured, only to be disappointed when he saw him still lying in bed, often asleep and seemingly powerless.

Peter lifted his left arm and checked the watch. He closed his eyes and thought, adding up the days and times, came to a conclusion that didn't fully satisfy him. He added up again and realized it must be correct. They had been gone for exactly six days. In ten hours, they had to be ready by the mountain.

He looked at Filip and said: "You have two hours to recover. And I really hope you're up for an eight-hour walk."

With light packing, they left *the west coast* and entered the forest that would lead them back to their mountain.

With heavy steps, Filip felt like an elephant caught in an unusually strong gravitational pull. He was still in bad shape, but the urgency of needing to reach the mountain in time gave him enough strength to overcome the painful, heavy steps, and his mind was active, his gaze focused. His goal was to make sure Peter got home to his brother on time.

Peter carried the backpack and Filip the revolver. The revolver was fully loaded. They had left earlier than planned and now they had nine hours. The journey up the mountain took them eight hours. On the return trip, they wouldn't be able to maintain the same pace, but hopefully, the extra hour they now had in reserve would make a difference.

They tried to stay as quiet as possible, making no unnecessary sounds, knowing that evil lurked somewhere out there. Filip's task was to keep watch and fire deadly projectiles if they were surprised by the monster. That was at least what they expected – that it would show up sooner or later. And if it did, they hoped it was the only one left, though they couldn't be entirely sure. There was a risk there could be more.

"Take some fruit," Peter said, holding out something that resembled a banana to Filip.

Peter tried to feed Filip as best as he could. During his time in the hospital bed, he had barely eaten anything. Now, he needed all the energy he could get. Peter's plan was to make sure he ate as much fruit as he could before opening the last can of beer sausage. No matter how full Filip was, he could always manage a couple of sausages. A bit like at Christmas; no matter how stuffed you are, there's always room for a plate of Ris à la Malta.

"Thanks, but that's enough. I'm about to burst," Filip replied, making a vomiting gesture.

"Okay. Not even a couple of sausages?"

"I know you're joking. The sausages must be finished by now."

"Actually, no. I saved a can. Can you manage?"

Filip stopped and sat down on a rock.

"A couple of sausages always go down. You know that."

Peter took off his backpack and fished out the last can of sausages. He punctured the lid with a knife and began to carve it open.

"What time is it?" Filip asked as he took the first sausage.

Peter checked the time and replied: "Three hours left. I think we're on track. And we really need to rest a little, too. At least you do."

"I actually feel better now than when we left," Filip said, stuffing the last of the sausage into his mouth. Then he stretched out his hand to Peter for more.

"Weren't you about to burst?"

"As I said. A few sausages always go down."

The scent of the sausages spread into the forest, and the light wind carried some of the scent molecules that could easily be picked up by a dog's sense of smell.

The wellst, who had been hiding in the forest since the chaos at the mountain, detected the smell of something interesting. Its mouth began to water immediately, and saliva dripped from its sharp canine teeth onto the moss.

It had managed to escape and had hidden from the two men with the incredibly loud and deadly device that had taken out its closest kindred. To it, they were now dead, and it had thought it was the last one remaining, but not everyone had died. One had woken up and wandered through the forest unnoticed, continuing until it reached the open ground, where it saw two lone humans that it considered an easy target, which turned out to be a mistake. The wellst was still hanging on the stone, pierced by an axe straight through its neck.

The larger group of wellsts, who had left the quarry after their escape in an attempt to return to their world, had succeeded. The villagers had been surprised by their entrance, but most had miraculously managed to stay clear of their chaotic path. When the mob finally made it underground to the open gate to their world, they were able to easily walk straight through the glowing, crackling hole without any resistance.

The wellst in the forest tried to trace the source of the scent. It moved slowly through the forest, and as the scent grew stronger, the urge for meat became more intense.

Now, it had only one goal in mind: to find the source of the delicious smell and then strike.

The last part of the journey had been completed, and they were now at the border between the forest and the wheat field. A little further ahead, they could see the hill, which, hopefully, would open for them. It had done so the last time they were on their way back, together with Mikael and Pernilla, so their hope was that it would do the same this time. At least, that was what they coldly counted on.

They had half an hour to spare, but if it took a little longer for the mountain to decide to open its gates, it wouldn't be the end of the world. They would still be closer in age to Mikael now than when they had first set off.

Peter began planning how to secure the rope. The suspension had to be designed in the best possible way to give them the speed and power required for a successful re-entry to their world. If the power and speed were too low, they would instead crash against the hard surface of the mountain.

Peter thought back to the earlier return trip, trying to calculate the weight of the four plus the sofa and what weight needed to be added to match the same weight as before. He could tie the rope higher up on the protruding tree above the mountain, but it wouldn't be enough; they needed more weight. Maybe a large stone? He felt time was running short if they were going to manage to get a stone large enough to make a difference.

"Filip! We need to hurry a bit. We've only got half an hour left, and we need to get the rope ready," he said, stressed.

"Isn't it just a matter of hanging it in the tree above?"

"We need more weight. We need to try tying a large stone; otherwise, there's a risk we won't make it through."

Filip, who had been too tired to think in those terms, still understood what Peter was getting at. They couldn't take any risks now that they were so close to their goal. And it would turn out that the stone wasn't the only problem they faced. Another problem, which they were completely unaware of at that moment, was a brutal killing machine weighing one hundred and ten kilos, standing between them and the gate back to Timmerlunda.

They reached the mountain, and Peter took the rope out of his backpack to climb up the hill and into the tree above.

"See if you can find a stone big enough to make a difference," he told Filip as he headed up the mountain.

Filip walked around, kicking a few stones that were sticking up from the ground. Eventually, he found one that might meet the criteria if he could manage to dig it up. He searched for his knife in Peter's backpack and began shoveling the dirt around the stone.

When Peter had looped the rope around one of the sturdier branches of the tree above, he lowered one end of the rope to the ground. Filip had managed to get the stone up, which surely weighed about twenty kilos, and had moved it to the spot below the tree. It turned out that the stone was perfectly suited for the purpose; its shape made it easy to secure it without risking it slipping off the rope, something that absolutely couldn't happen.

Filip tied the stone to the rope and lifted it to the perfect pendulum height while Peter fastened the other end around the branch. He then climbed down and stood next to Filip to admire their setup.

"This should work," he said to Filip, who agreed.

At that moment, there was a crackling sound at the bottom of the mountain wall in front of them.

"Damn, it's happening now!" Filip screamed.

"Talk about timing. But we're not quite done with the pendulum. We need to stretch it too."

Quickly as a flash, Peter grabbed the other rope from the backpack and tied one end just above the stone. Filip pushed the pendulum toward the tree while Peter tied the firing rope.

"That's enough," Filip said. "Now we need to climb."

Now, the wall gave off a deafening crackling sound and lit up with all its might. A welcome, magnificent spectacle that both Peter and Filip had been waiting for a long time. Finally, the time had come. They were going home again, home to Mikael and Pernilla, to reunite with them.

They climbed up the rope and straddled above the tied stone. Peter was ready with the knife, and they started counting down.

They stared into the blinding, illuminated wall in front of them, and Peter thought he saw a person standing in the light. Half-blinded by the light, he thought he saw the outline of someone standing between them and the wall. He first thought it was a hallucination, but when Filip shouted, "Damn, there's something there. Do you see it?" he realized what it was.

"Do you have the revolver?" he shouted to Filip. "It's the monster!"

"Still down there," Filip shouted back. "Cut the rope. We might miss it. It's our only chance. We need to get through. NOW!"

Peter cut the rope, and they quickly moved toward the mountain.

In front of them, they saw the light from the mountain wall approaching. They also saw the wellst stretching out its powerful, enormous arms to catch them. Moments later, they felt something hit their outstretched legs. Something meaty. Then they sank into the light and flew out through the other side, landing straight into the now-decayed remains of a strange wooden sofa.

Behind them, they heard a gargling roar that Peter recognized from the day in the field when he was almost certain that his best friend Filip had been killed by the monster.

They slowly turned around, prepared for the worst. The upper part of the wellst was hanging out through the mountain wall.

Chapter 16

Mikael woke up early on the Saturday morning of June 22, 2002. He rubbed the sleep from his eyes and sat up in bed. He looked down at the love of his life, still deep in her beauty sleep despite the absence of the seven types of flowers that were traditionally picked the day before Midsummer Eve to be placed under the pillow during the night. An old tradition to meet a lover.

Pernilla didn't need any flowers; she already had Mikael.

It was unusual for Mikael to wake up before Pernilla. But this morning, he had been awakened by a premonition, elated by a nearly euphoric feeling. He understood that there could only be one event capable of making him feel this way.

His brother's return.

He stayed in bed for a long time, soaking in the sensation, wondering if it could even be true. Had Peter returned? Why else would he have this feeling? Ten years had almost passed, and sometime from this summer onward, it was planned that he and Filip would return. So why not?

After an hour, Pernilla woke up. She was surprised that Mikael was already up, but when he told her about his premonition, she understood that it would have been impossible for him to fall back asleep after that.

At breakfast, Mikael was silent and withdrawn. Pernilla made no attempt to interrupt his thoughts. She thought that he would get over it soon, because after breakfast, they were going to Pernilla's parents' house to celebrate Midsummer. That would take his mind off things.

Mikael's parents would also come to celebrate, as they had for the past years. Mikael wondered if this year, like all the others, would end with his mother bursting into tears. The absence of Peter was still too overwhelming, and she no longer had high hopes that he would return. Mikael always had to comfort her and try to convince her that he would come back because that's what he had promised!

Their parents had made sure to keep Peter's apartment despite the uncertainty. Mikael, who had started working right after finishing middle school, moved in with Pernilla and took over the apartment after his first paycheck that year.

One problem that both Mikael and Pernilla had faced since returning from the monster world was identifying themselves and proving their existence—convincing an authority or similar institution that what had happened had actually happened, like when they had to return to school or when Mikael applied for a job, or when he had to sign the documents to take over the apartment.

So far, it had worked out. It might have been because the person involved eventually got tired of their unbelievable story, but they also knew they would have to deal with the uncertainty for a while longer. But later, after a few years, when they grew older, it would hopefully fade away because it would become harder to determine their real age.

Mikael thought Pernilla looked incredibly beautiful in her new white summer dress when they left the apartment. Her wonderfully sculpted face and her long, brownish, beautiful hair hanging down her back radiated a beauty hard to resist. Mikael felt incredibly lucky that they had met that summer, even though it had been in a completely different world. Only one thing could heighten that feeling. His twin brother Peter returned.

They would take their time walking the two kilometers to her parents' house, which on this day included a detour around the nearby fields to pick flowers for a wreath. They had left in good time and weren't in a hurry. Dinner wouldn't be served until twelve, and it was only eleven now.

As they stood by one of the flower-rich ditches, in twisting a daisy into Pernilla's wreath, Mikael suddenly lifted his gaze unconsciously and then let go of the wreath, which fell to the ground.

Pernilla observed him as he stood there frozen and initially wondered what had happened. But when she turned her head, she saw what had made Mikael unreachable: a little further down the gravel road, heading toward them, were two people she thought she recognized.

Chapter 17

The wellst struck and flailed with its arms in an attempt to break free. Peter and Filip sat paralyzed, watching until it stopped moving. The thought crossed Peter's mind later in the day whether the monster's legs had flailed around in the same way on the other side, but he dismissed the thought as quickly as it came.

"What do we do with it?" Peter asked.

"Ah, let it hang. The forest is probably full of hungry animals. It won't be long before it's eaten, you'll see."

"That's probably true," Peter said with a disgusted expression. "What do you think would have happened if it had made it all the way through?"

"Don't think about that now, Peter. We've made it home. The sun is shining, and the weather is nice. What more could one wish for?"

"Yes, now we know this. I think we should go home," Peter said, tearing his gaze away from the monster.

"I wonder if we've come back to the right year," Filip said thoughtfully, looking at Peter.

"According to your watch and our calculations, we have. But we can't be completely sure until we've confirmed it."

"Your calculation, you mean," Filip said, correcting him and giving Peter a small smile.

"Yes, yes. My calculation." They tore off their heavy outer clothing and shoved it under a pine tree, then set off toward familiar ground, toward Timmerlunda, where they hoped to be pleasantly surprised by learning what year it was. They, of course, had no idea it was Midsummer's Eve morning. And the odds of returning on that exact day of the year were something they would laugh about later in the evening.

The sun was warming nicely as they rounded the lake and followed the gravel road the last stretch into Timmerlunda. A little further ahead, they saw a couple standing at the roadside. Peter was happy to see real people again. Although the underground people they had met were kind and friendly, it was still nice to see a couple of real earth dwellers again.

As they approached the couple, Filip whispered something to Peter without really thinking all the way through. Maybe it was because he was tired and worn out, maybe because his thoughts were still in a completely different world. He just blurted it out: "He looks like you, the one over there along the road."

Peter stopped and placed his hand on Filip's chest to stop him. Then he said with a broad smile on his lips: "And she looks very much like Pernilla." They looked at each other for a moment before quickening their pace toward the couple they believed to be Mikael and Pernilla.

Pernilla smiled as she took Mikael's hand and followed him toward the two approaching people, who they were now sure were Peter and Filip. Mikael couldn't hold back and shouted, "Peter," and started running. Pernilla kept up the same pace, refusing to let go. She didn't want to miss Mikael's and Peter's reunion for anything in the world.

"Micke," Peter shouted back, and now they were only a few meters away from each other.

A couple of hours ago, they had been an unfathomable distance apart, living in two completely different worlds. In one world, Mikael had waited ten years to reunite with his brother. In the other, Peter had been separated from Mikael for barely a week—but every single day, he had longed for him, worried that he might not succeed in making it back to Timmerlunda.

They had barely managed to escape through the mountain without the monster catching them. It had been sheer luck that they had only met it slightly off to the side. Had they taken a direct hit to the chest, their speed would have slowed just enough to prevent them from generating the force needed to break through. They would have collapsed in a heap on the ground—along with the monster. And who knew what would happen then?

But none of that mattered now. They were back. Peter and Filip.

The moment they saw each other, they threw themselves into a huge hug and burst into hysterical laughter. They couldn't believe it. They had made it. They were together again, and they were the same age. Peter and Filip had managed to set everything right, and they were overwhelmed with happiness. They laughed so hard they thought they might never stop. Eventually, though, their laughter began to taper off. And then came the questions.

Mikael and Pernilla were eager to know how their journey had gone and whether the other world had still been the same. Peter first had to remind them that only a week had passed since they left—not ten years. Then he and Filip recounted their adventures: the underground people they had met and the monsters that had nearly put an end to their expedition.

Mikael and Pernilla, in turn, shared what had happened at home while Peter and Filip were away. As it turned out, quite a bit had changed. For one, Mikael and Pernilla had moved into Peter's apartment together—they were now officially a couple. Peter grinned, saying he had known all along that it was only a matter of time.

That evening, they all went to Pernilla's parents' house to celebrate Midsummer. It turned out to be a Midsummer they would never forget.

Mrs. Svensson had a few more fainting spells, just like the last time they had returned from what she dramatically called "the land of the dead." Mr. Svensson, on the other hand, took it in stride. He was most curious about what had happened and how they had managed to make it through once again. At this point, nothing surprised him anymore. With Mikael, Peter, and Filip together, anything was possible.

The day passed in a blur of celebration—herring and potatoes for lunch, afternoon games, and a proper barbecue in the evening. Later, the four of them took a walk through Timmerlunda, eventually making their way up to the lookout hill in the park. There, they sat in a row, quietly watching the sun dip below the horizon.

For a long time, they simply sat in silence, each lost in their own thoughts about everything they had been through. Then, Mikael broke the quiet.

"I've been thinking about something," he said. "How do you think time works in the monster's world? I mean, the world they came from?"

Peter turned to him. "What do you mean?"

"Well," Mikael continued, "here, time moves fast. And in the other world—the one we were just in—time moved slowly. But what if, in the monster's world, time moves even faster than here? What if we could get there? Then we could—"

"Stop! Stop right now!"

The other three shouted in unison and tackled Mikael to the ground.

"That's enough!"

www.ingramcontent.com/pod-product-compliance
Lightning Source LLC
Chambersburg PA
CBHW040858010826
48978CB00013BA/1078